"I'm not at all your type."

"Why do you say that?"

"It's obvious." Lacey set the bowls down on the table with brisk efficiency. "You went out with the party girls, whereas I was—"

"Too good for me."

"What?" She looked up in obvious surprise.

"You heard me. I was the bad boy with the souped-up truck and mediocre grades. You were an honor student with goals and a curfew."

"Okay, so we were different, but I never thought I was too good for you, Tucker."

"No, you wouldn't think that, because you're a nice person. But I knew it. It didn't stop me from kissing you, though. I saw my opportunity and took advantage of you being sad and vulnerable." He rubbed the back of his neck, where tension had gathered. He hadn't meant to start confessing his sins, but now that he had... "I shouldn't have kissed you that night."

"So you regret it?"

He met her gaze and something in the depths of those blue eyes demanded complete honesty. "No," he said softly. "I'm not that noble."

IT'S CHRISTMAS, COWBOY

SONS OF CHANCE

Vicki Lewis Thompson

Ocean Dance Press

ISBN: 978-1-63803-955-6

Ocean Dance Press LLC
PO Box 69901
Oro Valley, AZ 85737

Visit the author's website at
VickiLewisThompson.com

1

A runaway horse and an approaching blizzard made for a bad combo, especially the afternoon before Christmas. Tucker Rankin's eyes watered as he gunned the snowmobile in an effort to catch Houdini, a black and white stallion with a taste for freedom. The roar of the snowmobile and the white rooster tail it created shattered the peace and quiet of a Wyoming landscape blanketed by last week's storm.

About two hours of daylight remained, and the blizzard could hit anytime. The black and white Paint might survive out here alone tonight, but then again, he might not. Meanwhile everyone at the Last Chance Ranch was gearing up for a festive holiday. Tucker knew all about ruined Christmas celebrations and was determined to save both the stallion and the day.

As the recent hire who didn't much care about Christmas, Tucker had volunteered to get all the Last Chance horses, including Houdini, into their stalls around noon in anticipation of the blizzard. He'd gone back to check on them about three and had come nose-to-nose with Houdini, who'd let himself out of his stall.

Tucker had grabbed for the horse's halter and missed as Houdini bolted through the open barn door. After making a quick call on his cell to the main house, Tucker had stuffed a sack of oats and a lead rope in the saddlebag of one of the ranch snowmobiles and headed off in pursuit of the stallion.

He cussed out the horse, but mostly he blamed himself. He should have anticipated the jail break, considering the stallion had done it before. Thank God he hadn't unlatched any of the other stalls, which was another one of his tricks.

Houdini could potentially earn thousands in stud fees for the Last Chance provided he didn't freeze his ass out here tonight. Jack Chance, who owned the Jackson Hole area ranch along with his two brothers Nick and Gabe and his widowed mother Sarah, had bought the two-year-old for a song because Houdini was untrained and rambunctious. His previous owner had meant to school him, but those plans had been sidetracked by various personal issues.

In the few weeks Houdini had spent at the Last Chance, he'd learned to tolerate a halter and a lead rope, but he had a long way to go before he could be used as a stud, let alone for cutting horse competitions. His natural curiosity and inventiveness made him a royal pain to deal with.

Tucker felt a certain kinship with the rowdy horse. He hadn't exactly been a model of responsible behavior, either. He'd partied all through high school and had seen no reason to stop doing that after graduation ten years ago. He'd worked just enough to stay solvent.

It was a dead-end street, and when Jack Chance had hired him back in September, they'd discussed Tucker's lack of focus. Tucker had promised he was ready to buckle down and make something of himself. Accidentally allowing Houdini to escape might be a forgivable offense, but Tucker didn't feel as if he had room to make mistakes. Retrieving the horse was his job.

Because he'd grown up in the area, he knew that the Last Chance prided itself on offering people and animals a fresh start. He and Houdini had come to the right place. Tucker appreciated that fact, but obviously the horse, after being allowed to do as he pleased for two years, did not.

At least his trail was easy to follow in the snow. That wouldn't be true in a blizzard, however, and flakes had begun swirling through the frigid air. Tucker's sheepskin coat wasn't enough protection from this kind of weather, even with the collar turned up.

He crammed his Stetson on tight and reached up to anchor it with a gloved hand whenever it threatened to blow off. He wished he'd picked up some goggles, but he'd been too intent on rescuing the horse to think of his own comfort. The moisture from his eyes turned his lashes to icicles, but that couldn't be helped.

Thank God the horse had stayed out in the open instead of running into the trees. Tucker needed to catch him before he changed his mind about that, because the snowmobile would be no use in the forested part of Chance land.

Pointing the snowmobile toward a small rise, Tucker hoped to get a glimpse of the horse. Sure enough, the black and white Paint galloped merrily through the meadow about two hundred yards ahead of him. The snow was deep enough to spray in all directions, but not deep enough to be dangerous and cause injuries. Houdini seemed to be having the time of his life.

Tucker stopped the snowmobile and gave a sharp whistle, knowing that was probably a waste of breath. True to form, Houdini didn't break stride. Fogging the air with some choice words, Tucker took off after him.

If the stakes hadn't been so high, Tucker would have enjoyed this chase. Houdini was the picture of carefree pleasure, his tail a waving flag signaling his delight at escaping the barn. Tucker understood the urge to throw off the traces. He'd done it often enough.

But reckless behavior had consequences. Last summer he'd ended up with a DUI after wrecking his truck. Only dumb luck had kept him from injuring or killing someone, and that wreck and subsequent DUI had been a wakeup call.

He'd always admired the Chance brothers, and going to work for them represented progress in his mind. He wanted their respect, and letting a valuable stallion escape was a step in the wrong direction. Recapturing Houdini was critical for the horse, but also for Tucker's self-confidence.

Now that he had the stallion in his sights, he felt better about the likelihood of catching him. Getting back might be a little tricky, though. Snow fell more rapidly with every second. It blocked most of the light and at times obscured his view of the racing horse.

Once he had the horse, he'd call the ranch and let them know his status. Ahead of them, a barbed wire fence came into view, which meant they'd traveled farther than he'd thought and were at the boundary of Chance land. He'd never ridden in this direction before.

That fence could be a huge problem. Houdini could jump it if he took a notion, and the snowmobile... couldn't. "Don't jump the damn fence," Tucker muttered under his breath. "Please."

Houdini galloped toward it as if he had every intention of doing that. Beyond the fence stood a small log cabin with lights on and a ribbon of smoke rising from the chimney. If they had a snowmobile parked in the outbuilding, he'd ask to borrow it if he had to.

But he'd rather capture the horse on this side of the fence and be done with it. He pushed the snowmobile faster, determined to reach Houdini before the horse made it to the fence. He concentrated so hard on that goal that he didn't notice a large rock jutting out of the snow until the snowmobile's runner found it.

Next thing he knew, he lay flat on his back in the snow, the wind knocked clean out of him. The blood roared in his ears as he struggled to breathe. What a fine mess. Houdini was probably over the fence and half a mile away by now. The snowmobile was silent, probably wrecked.

Then a black and white muzzle appeared above him. A blast of steamy air hit his face as Houdini snorted.

Relief flooded through Tucker as he grabbed the horse's halter. "Gotcha."

* * *

Lacey Evans had heard the approaching snowmobile and hoped it wouldn't be anyone coming to check on her. She was doing fine out here by herself, thank you very much. The cabin was filled with the aroma of stew simmering, bread baking, and a fire crackling.

The cabin's owner had seemed nervous about renting to her after she'd explained that her male companion wouldn't be joining her as planned. She'd finally convinced the owner that her Forest Service job made her more qualified than most men to spend a few days alone in an isolated cabin. And that definitely included her piece-of-crap ex-boyfriend Lenny.

Going to the window, she'd peered through the falling snow and figured out that a cowboy on a snowmobile was chasing a black and white horse on the far side of the barbed wire fence. One of the Chance boys' Paints had apparently escaped. She watched the chase with interest.

But when the snowmobile flipped, she shoved her feet into her boots, pulled a stocking cap over her head, and snatched up her coat. That cowboy could be in trouble.

Thank goodness he didn't seem to be badly hurt. By the time she reached the fence, he was on his feet and had somehow captured the horse. The snowmobile didn't look particularly good, though. It had landed upside down, and one runner was bent all to hell.

She took the time to put on her insulated gloves. "Are you okay?" she called out.

"I'm fine." His voice was tight with strain. "I... whoa, boy. Whoa!" The horse whinnied and tried to rear, but the cowboy hung on with both gloved hands and brought the horse's head back down.

She admired his determination to keep a grip on the horse, which looked like the devil's own mount as it blew steam from its nostrils and pawed at the ground. "Should I call somebody?"

"That's okay. I have my cell." He looked from the horse to the snowmobile and back at her. "But he's a handful. It'd be a help if you could fetch the lead rope out of the snowmobile's saddlebag. He usually settles down once he's on the lead."

"I can do that." She'd also pick up his hat, which was lying in the snow. She knew how cowboys felt about their hats.

Parting the barbed wire carefully, she leaned down and stepped between the strands. "Will he try to kick me?"

"No." The cowboy gulped in air. "He's not mean. Just likes to be in control. I'll feel better once I have a lead rope on him."

Lacey retrieved the fallen hat before crouching down and pulling the rope out of the saddlebag. "And then what?"

"I... don't know." The snow fell faster and he muttered under his breath.

She could guess the nature of those mutterings as she handed him the rope and his hat. Anyone from this area knew that Wyoming blizzards could be deadly.

She thought he was local because he looked vaguely familiar. He wasn't a Chance, though. She'd grown up here and knew what each of the Chance men looked like. Still, something about this cowboy was familiar. She'd seen those green eyes and dark hair before.

"Thanks." He put on his hat and clipped the rope to the horse's halter as the snow swirled and gusted around them.

"I hope you're not thinking of riding back."

He greeted that with a short laugh. "He's never been ridden."

"You can wait it out in my cabin, but that doesn't solve the horse issue."

He glanced from the horse to her cabin. "What's in the outbuilding?"

"My Jeep." She raised her voice to be heard over the howl of the wind. "But we can't risk driving in this."

"I know." He secured his hat with one gloved hand when it started to blow off. "But can we stable him there for the night?"

"I guess." She considered the logistics of getting through the fence. "You got wire cutters?"

"Nope."

"Then I'll get mine."

"You have wire cutters?"

"I work for the Forest Service." She started to walk away and turned back as curiosity got the better of her. "Do I know you from somewhere?"

"I grew up here. The name's Tucker Rankin."

"Tucker?" Her eyes widened. "I'm Lacey. Lacey Evans. Jackson Hole High School."

"I'll be damned."

"Small world. I'll be back as quick as I can." She hurried toward the fence and ducked through the strands of barbed wire.

Tucker Rankin. She hadn't thought about him in years. Hurrying toward the cabin's outbuilding, she sorted through her recollections of Tucker. He'd been a bad boy back then, too wild for her, although she'd secretly found him very sexy.

But one vivid memory surfaced. She'd gone to the Christmas formal their senior year against her better judgment. But a sweet, nerdy boy had asked her and she hadn't had the heart to turn him down.

Normally she just didn't do Christmas. Her mother had died when she was fifteen, and her mom had been the person who'd made the holiday special. After that it had been less painful to ignore Christmas completely.

Her dad had remarried when she was seventeen, and although Lacey had tried valiantly to appreciate her stepmother's efforts, the lady wasn't the most sensitive person in the world. She'd crudely trampled on all Lacey's mother's traditions.

A pre-lit artificial tree and battery-operated candles appeared. Cranberry and popcorn garlands were proclaimed too messy. Gifts were opened Christmas Eve instead of Christmas morning. Any reference to Santa was labeled a childish fantasy.

Lacey's sister and brother had adapted, but Lacey, being the oldest, had the strongest memories of pine-scented boughs, flickering beeswax candles, hand-strung garlands, and wrapped packages under the tree on Christmas morning. She'd never made the adjustment. Still, she'd agreed to be Arnold's date for the Christmas formal.

Just her luck, the dance committee had decorated a huge evergreen that filled the gym with its fragrance, and they'd continued the torture by placing beeswax votives around the room. When Lacey had slipped outside, tearful with nostalgia, Tucker had been there, too, enjoying a forbidden cigarette.

He'd offered her his coat, and they'd exchanged views on Christmas. She'd found out that his mom had died on Christmas Eve when he was twelve, which was a way worse situation than hers. He didn't celebrate the holiday anymore, either, but a girl had asked him to the formal.

Turned out she'd done it to make another guy jealous, and her ex had arrived to claim her five minutes earlier. Tucker wasn't having a particularly good time at this Christmas event, either. They'd shared their holiday angst, both past and present, that night.

They'd also shared a heated kiss that had scared the living daylights out of her. Rattled by the lust he'd inspired with one kiss, she'd returned his coat and dashed back inside. They'd never talked again.

After taking her wire cutters out of the Jeep, she quickly assessed the interior of the outbuilding that doubled as a garage. A horse would fit in there next to her Jeep, which was old and beat up. A few kicks from a horse's hooves wouldn't be noticed.

Inviting Tucker into her cabin to spend the night wasn't quite so convenient. She'd planned to spend three days there with Lenny. Until a week ago, BTB (Before the Bimbo) she and Lenny had been practically engaged, and she'd intended to take a stab at celebrating Christmas on a small scale.

A one-bedroom hideaway had seemed adequate for a couple. But she and Tucker were not a couple, and there was only one bed. He was too tall to fit comfortably on the couch, and she hated to make him sleep on the floor when she had no sleeping bag or air mattress.

But the blizzard was upon them and he had to get in out of it. They'd work out the details later. She lowered her head and leaned into the wind as she returned to the fence. Tucker stood like a marble statue beside the horse, and Lacey wondered if he held himself rigid so he wouldn't betray any weakness with an unmanly shiver.

"I called the ranch." His lips looked a little blue and his eyelashes and eyebrows were crusted with snow. "I said I'd wait out the storm here. I explained you were an old high school friend."

"Perfect." She had a little trouble manipulating the wire cutters with her thick gloves on, but she managed to cut both strands and pull them back, creating a decent-sized opening. "Let's get going. It's cold out here."

His chuckle became a cough. "I noticed. Oh, wait. There's a sack of oats in the saddlebag. I'll lead Houdini if you'll grab the oats. He'll need something to eat."

"Right." She moved quickly through the opening in the fence and over to the snowmobile, which at the rate it was snowing, would soon be covered. Oats in hand, she followed Tucker through the fence and across what had been a defined road an hour ago. Soon it would be obliterated, too.

She dashed around both horse and man to open the double doors into the outbuilding. The cold must be having a calming effect on the Paint, because he walked into the shelter without protest. Maybe he realized that it wasn't so much fun being outside in a blizzard.

Lacey gestured to the heater designed to prevent engines from freezing. "This should help keep him warmer, too."

"He'll appreciate that." Tucker brushed the snow from Houdini's back before glancing around the makeshift garage. "Do you think I could use that bucket in the corner to feed him some oats?"

"Don't see why not." She retrieved the bucket and handed it to him, along with the small sack of oats. "Will this be enough?"

"I'll only give him half for now, in case I need to ration it." He opened the sack and poured some into the bucket while managing to hold it away from Houdini. Once he set it down, the horse shoved his nose deep into the bucket and began munching. The bucket rattled against the outbuilding's cement floor.

Lacey couldn't imagine that little bit of oats would satisfy an animal of Houdini's size. "I brought apples, and I have some carrots left over from the stew I made, if you want to give him those later on."

"Stew?" Tucker was so obviously trying to control his shivers as he smiled at her. "God, that s-sounds wonderful."

"You're frozen, aren't you?"

"Pretty much."

"Then let's get inside and warm you up." She'd thought it was an innocent remark, but as they closed the horse inside the outbuilding and she led the way into the cabin, she thought about how she could warm him up, and it had nothing to do with stew.

That kiss had replayed itself in her mind quite a few times since she'd found out who he was. He'd had a reputation in high school as a skilled lover, and if that kiss had been a sample, his reputation had been well deserved. For several months after that kiss, she'd had potent dreams involving naked bodies writhing on soft sheets.

And here she was, snowbound with the object of her teenage fantasies. She blew out an impatient breath. What nonsense. For all she knew Tucker was married and had a couple of kids.

Once they were inside the warm cabin and had started divesting themselves of their jackets and gloves, she glanced at him. "I suppose someone will be really disappointed if you don't show up for Christmas Eve."

He hooked his coat on a peg by the door and followed it with his hat. "Can't say that they will." He turned to gaze at her. "Are you out here by yourself?"

"Yes." So he was single, apparently. "It just turned out that way." She tried not to gawk, but damn, he was even better looking now than he had been in high school. His features were more chiseled, and the hint of a beard gave him a rugged look that stirred up butterflies in her stomach.

His glance swept the cabin's living room and open kitchen. "No holiday decorations, I see."

"Nope." And he smelled good, too — the musky scent of a man who worked with animals. She hadn't realized how much she liked that earthy aroma on a man.

"I'm going to take a wild guess that you're not into this holiday any more than you were years ago when we had that conversation outside the school gym."

"So you remember that." She met his gaze. It wasn't the conversation she was focusing on, but what had followed the conversation. The mouth she'd kissed long ago looked much the same except for some added smile lines bracketing his firm lips.

"Yeah, I do remember, in fact." A telltale flicker in his green eyes contradicted his casual tone.

Her heart rate increased another notch. She'd bet money he was thinking about that kiss, too. "Well, you're right. I still don't much like Christmas. How about you?"

"Can't say it's my favorite time of year."

She kept her attention on his face, but she was very aware of the snug fit of his western shirt. The soft blue plaid revealed muscles honed by ranch work. "I'll bet the Last Chance goes all out."

He rolled his eyes. "You have no idea. Fifteen-foot tree in the living room, holly and pine boughs on the banister going upstairs, red velvet bows on everything that doesn't move. They've even decorated the damned barn."

She ignored a sharp pang of longing. Being surrounded by that kind of festive atmosphere would only make her sad. "You won't find that here."

"Good. Maybe it's just as well we ended up together tonight." He smiled. "We're birds of a feather."

Oh, yeah. She remembered that smile — the one that went from boyish to seductive in zero-point-five seconds. Heat spiraled through her system. Ten years ago she hadn't allowed herself to be swept away by his animal magnetism. But tonight, after being dumped last week by the man she'd thought she'd eventually marry, all bets were off.

2

Lacey Evans. Whenever he'd thought of her in the years since high school, which had been more times than he cared to admit, he'd pictured her with a stodgy but successful husband and a couple of cute kids. Once again she'd be totally out of reach, as she had been when they were in high school.

Instead, against all odds, he was standing in this cozy cabin with her. She didn't seem to be attached to a guy, let alone have any kids. She hadn't known he would show up, so the setting she'd created had nothing to do with him.

But she couldn't have planned a more tempting scenario than a welcoming fire, a home-cooked meal, and the prospect of spending time with a woman he'd wanted desperately when he was eighteen. Who needed Christmas?

The years had been good to her. Her honey-colored hair was slightly darker, now, and she wore it shorter, too, an easy-care mop of caramel curls. Those curls were tousled by the stocking cap she'd pulled off, and he had the urge to comb her hair into place with his fingers.

Her blue eyes were no longer so wide and endearingly innocent. After she'd run from his kiss that night, her cheeks bright pink, he'd decided that he'd been French-kissing a virgin. But there was nothing virginal in her frank appraisal of him now. The glow in those amazing eyes told him that if he kissed her again, she wouldn't run.

The possibility heated his blood, and suddenly, he wasn't the least bit cold. She'd had that effect on him from the first day he'd glimpsed her walking down the hall at Jackson Hole High, her snug sweater and jeans showing off a sweetly curved figure. He'd thought he'd died and gone to heaven the one and only time he'd held her in his arms.

When she'd ended that unforgettable kiss, she'd returned his coat. He'd left it off in hopes cold air would deflate his penis enough for him to walk to his truck and drive home. The wait had seemed like hours.

He liked to think he had more control these days, but apparently not when it came to Lacey. She still favored snug jeans and close-fitting sweaters. Today's sweater was green, which signaled full speed ahead to his eager package.

Tucker decided, in the name of his own self-respect, to show some restraint. Although he wasn't proud of it, he'd engaged in some meaningless sex over the years. When life was one big party, a guy didn't much care who he slept with if the woman was willing and warm.

But Lacey was different. She wasn't just some girl he'd met in a cowboy bar. Yeah, he wanted her, but he didn't have to act on that urge. Instead, he could distract himself by concentrating on a different kind of hunger.

He glanced over at the stove, the source of mouthwatering aromas. "I don't know much about cooking, but is there any chance that stew is ready to eat?"

She smiled. "Yep. Your timing is excellent."

"Dumb luck." But he'd had quite a bit of luck lately, especially landing the job at the Last Chance. He was beginning to wonder if Houdini's escape had been an example of good luck disguised as potential disaster. "What can I do to help?"

"Not a thing. If you want to wash up, there's soap and towels in the bathroom." She gestured toward a short hall. "First door on your left."

"Thanks. Good plan." He probably smelled of horse. Some women liked that, but he didn't know if Lacey did or not. He headed down the hall, his boots clicking on the hardwood floor of the cabin.

The bathroom was plain — white fixtures and a tub shower with a white curtain. Tucker caught a glimpse of himself in the medicine cabinet mirror and winced. Hat hair, red nose, five-o'clock shadow. He must have imagined that glint of interest in her eyes. What woman would be attracted to *that*?

Rolling back his sleeves, he turned on the water and picked up the soap. He couldn't do anything about the five-o'clock shadow, but soap and warm water would make him feel more presentable. Then he noticed that the soap was imbedded with an image of Santa Claus.

The cabin's owners might have left it, but the lack of frills everywhere else made that unlikely.

Probably somebody had given it to Lacey and she was practical enough to make use of it. He could help her with that.

He lathered up, scrubbing his face and hands until they tingled. The soap smelled like candy canes. He hadn't thought of those in awhile. His mom used to buy a lot of them to decorate the tree because they were affordable.

His dad had thought the whole tree thing was a waste of money, but his mom had insisted on having one every year. She and Tucker had strung popcorn and made chains of construction paper. That had all ended when she died.

No point in dredging up those memories, though, especially when he was with a woman who also ignored the holiday except for some soap she was trying to use up. He splashed cold water on his face, grabbed a towel, and dried off. Then he finger-combed his hair as best he could.

He walked back into the kitchen, where a loaf of what looked like homemade bread sat on a cutting board in the middle of the table. Lacey was dishing stew into a couple of generously sized bowls. The light caught in her caramel curls as she glanced up and smiled at him.

His breath stalled at the beauty of the scene, at the beauty of her, all flushed from the heat of the stove. Or maybe her extra color had something to do with him being there. That was a happy prospect.

"This looks wonderful. Thank you." Then he had a thought. "Listen, if you feed me now, are you going to have enough supplies for your stay?"

"Oh, yeah." She laughed as she opened the refrigerator, which was stuffed. "I read the weather reports and decided to be prepared for anything. As I said, I can probably help feed your horse if it comes to that."

"He's not exactly my horse. I just work there. But I'm relieved to know you stocked up."

"The good news is I'm loaded with provisions. The bad news is the provisions are everything I like, but you may not like the same things."

"Beggars can't be choosers. I'm grateful for whatever you're willing to share."

Her quick glance in his direction told him that she'd taken that in a way he hadn't meant. God, he hoped he hadn't offended her. "Sorry. That didn't come out right."

She became very busy ladling out the stew. "Don't worry about it. I mean, we had that one silly moment together after the winter formal, but I'm not at all your type."

"Why do you say that?"

"It's obvious." She set the bowls down on the table with brisk efficiency. "You went out with the party girls, whereas I was—"

"Too good for me."

"What?" She looked up in obvious surprise.

"You heard me. I was the bad boy with the souped-up truck and mediocre grades. You were an honor student with goals and a curfew."

"Okay, so we were different, but I never thought I was too good for you, Tucker."

"No, you wouldn't think that, because you're a nice person. But I knew it. It didn't stop me from kissing you, though. I saw my opportunity and took advantage of you being sad and vulnerable." He rubbed the back of his neck, where tension had gathered. He hadn't meant to start confessing his sins, but now that he had... "I shouldn't have kissed you that night."

"So you regret it?"

He met her gaze and something in the depths of those blue eyes demanded complete honesty. "No," he said softly. "I'm not that noble."

"Well, that's a relief." The corners of her mouth turned up in a saucy smile.

He stared at her. He still hadn't quite made the adjustment from the virginal Lacey to the more self-assured woman standing in front of him. Once he did, he'd have a helluva time keeping his hands to himself.

She gestured toward the table as if ready to change the subject. "As I was saying, the supplies are all things I like. That means your choice of beverage is coffee, water, or wine. Most cowboys I know prefer beer."

He was more than ready to change the subject. Although he did prefer beer, he'd been known to drink wine. But he wasn't going to use up whatever she'd brought for herself. That would be rude. "I'll just drink water."

"You're sure? I'm having wine and unless you hate it, you're welcome to have some with me."

"I don't hate it, but I wouldn't feel right using up your—"

"Oh, for heaven's sake." She pulled two goblets out of the cupboard and set one by each plate. "Besides, I think we need to toast."

"To Christmas?" He had a tough time believing she'd want to do that.

"No, to meeting again after all these years."

"Oh." He was flattered that she'd count it a toasting occasion. "I guess we could toast to that."

"It's quite a coincidence, don't you think?"

"I do. It took a runaway horse and a wrecked snowmobile to accomplish it."

She opened the wine and poured each of them a glass. "And a slimeball. Let's not forget my worthless ex."

"Husband?" His high spirits plummeted. He should have known she hadn't intended to be out here all by herself, that a man had originally been part of the deal.

"Boyfriend." She picked up her wineglass and handed one to him. "Fortunately that's all he ever was."

Tucker understood now why she'd looked at him with interest. With his playboy reputation, he had a history of attracting women on the rebound. That kind of relationship wasn't built to last. Either the woman moved on after she felt better about herself or she went back to her ex.

Usually that was fine with him, because he was careful not to get invested. But he didn't feel like being Lacey's rebound guy. She held a special place in his heart, and he didn't want to tarnish that memory.

Still, he knew his lines in situations like this. "Your ex is obviously a loser if he let you go."

"Thank you. I agree." She lifted her glass. "To old friends."

"To old friends." He touched his glass to hers and drank. But as he lowered the glass, honesty made him speak up. "We weren't really friends in high school, Lacey."

"Depends on how you define it. I thought we became friends that night outside the gym."

"I guess." If she hadn't run away, they would have become more than friends. He was glad they hadn't. He'd have enough trouble keeping this night from veering toward sex when all he'd done was kiss her. If she hadn't left, he would have continued the seduction he'd begun with that kiss. He'd been eighteen and flooded with hormones.

Now he was twenty-eight, and still somewhat hormone driven, but not to the exclusion of all reason. When necessary he could summon a little common sense. Lacey was a woman he could fall for, and yet she'd been recently dumped. That combo meant she was off limits.

She waved a hand at the table. "Let's eat."

"Good idea." Tucker hadn't been particularly polished when he'd arrived at the Last Chance, but Sarah Chance was a stickler for good manners. He'd learned that any cowboy who worked at the ranch had better know the fundamentals or risk losing his job.

Setting down his wine glass, he rounded the table to pull out Lacey's chair.

"How gallant." She accepted the gesture with a smile and slipped gracefully into the chair.

As he scooted it forward, he breathed in the scent of candy canes and woman. Obviously she'd used that soap, too. He wanted to bury his nose in the curve of her neck and nibble on her earlobe. But that wouldn't be wise.

He took a seat opposite her, unfolded the paper napkin she'd provided and settled it on his lap. Outside the wind rattled the windowpanes, which made their dinner seem all the more cozy in comparison. The food smelled delicious, but hungry as he was, he waited for Lacey to start eating.

She began by picking up a serrated knife and slicing off a couple pieces of bread. The scent of it burst forth, beckoning him with a yeasty aroma that reminded him of good sex. He'd always thought food and lovemaking went together.

He set that notion firmly aside. "I didn't know you could cook."

"You still don't." She held out the breadboard. "For all you know, this tastes like Styrofoam."

He picked up the heel, bit into its soft center, and closed his eyes. Heaven.

"It must be all right."

"Mm." He glanced at her and nodded enthusiastically as he chewed.

"Fortunately my mom taught me to bake when I was a kid. I picked up basic cooking skills when I realized my dad was hopeless in the kitchen. Of course, now he has Helen."

Grasping at a subject that didn't involve naked bodies, he asked about her family as they both dug into the beef stew.

She chose to ignore her dad and Helen and talk about her siblings, instead. Kathy, four years younger than she was, had married and moved to Ohio. Steven was finishing a degree in engineering at the University of Wyoming. Even given Lacey's reluctance to celebrate Christmas, Tucker was surprised she wasn't with her family right now, and he said as much.

"I know it's not very evolved of me, but I grit my teeth whenever I have to watch the way Helen celebrates Christmas," she said. "So I keep my participation to a minimum. This year I used Lenny as an excuse. I told them he was likely to propose over the holiday, and that I thought the two of us should create our own special memories by renting this cute little cabin for a week during Christmas."

"Do they know Lenny's not here with you?"

"No. I decided when he bailed that I'd keep that info to myself and come out here alone. The irony is that I really had planned to have a semi-normal Christmas with him. He likes the holiday, so I was going to make an effort for his sake, sort of to prove I could."

Tucker put down his spoon. "What happened with Lenny?" He cared about her broken heart and was willing to let her talk it out. That didn't mean he had to make it all better with some good sex, though. There was such a thing as self-preservation.

"Two weeks ago he met somebody he liked better, somebody who didn't have — to use his phrase — my baggage."

Tucker had the immediate urge to clean the guy's clock. "Hell, everyone has baggage."

"I know." She sliced off two more pieces of bread and gestured for him to take one. "Maybe Lenny and Suzanne have matching luggage tags."

"Could be, but I'll bet they're attached to the most boring suitcases in the world, that black nylon kind a million other people have."

She smiled at him. "I like to think so."

"Whereas yours has style. It might even be purple."

That made her laugh. "Okay, that's my new slogan. *I may have baggage, but I carry it with style.*"

"You do, Lacey." He picked up his wine glass and lifted it in her direction. The sparkle was back in her blue eyes, and he liked seeing that. "You definitely do."

"Thanks, Tucker." She lifted her glass, too. "So do you."

She wouldn't think so if she knew what a screw-up he'd been recently. He wished now that he'd made more of himself in the years since they'd last met. If she worked for the Forest Service, she'd probably earned a degree before landing that job.

Then something occurred to him. "Did you go into forestry because of the trees?" Once the words were out of his mouth, he realized how stupid that sounded. Didn't everybody who majored in forestry love trees? "I mean, because you used to love the evergreens at Christmastime."

She paused, a spoonful of stew halfway to her mouth, and stared at him. "You are the only person who's made that connection. I didn't realize it myself until recently, when I started thinking about celebrating a real Christmas here with Lenny and knew I'd want a real tree."

"But you gave up the idea when he..." He wasn't sure what term to use that wouldn't be insulting.

"When he dumped me. You can say it. It's the truth, after all. And a girl who's been dumped right before Christmas usually isn't ready to deck the halls with boughs of holly, if you get my drift." She continued eating her stew.

"Maybe that's exactly the time to do it."

She stopped eating and gazed at him. "How so?"

"You were going to celebrate Christmas for Lenny's sake, right?"

"Yeah, but obviously I picked the wrong guy to jump-start my Christmas spirit. He's pushed me right back into bah-humbug territory."

Tucker recognized that kind of thinking. For years he'd seen himself as a victim of circumstance. Hearing it coming from Lacey was unsettling. Funny how much easier it was to figure out what other people should do to make themselves happy.

"Tucker, why are you looking at me like that?"

"I'm just wondering why you'd break out the decorations for a guy, but not for yourself. Why let his dumb decisions keep you from celebrating if you have the urge to do it?"

She frowned. "I'm not saying I wanted to, but I thought it was time to see if I could, because depriving him of the holiday wasn't fair."

"Is it fair to deprive yourself? When we talked outside the gym, I got the impression that you used to love Christmas, especially the way your mother celebrated it." And so had he. His words were as much directed at himself as at her.

Her expression softened. "I did love it back then, but I can't recreate that kind of Christmas because my mom was such a huge part of it, and she's gone. I thought maybe I'd try for some new traditions with Lenny, but bravely forging my own rituals without anyone to share them seems a little desperate and pathetic."

"I get that. I've thought exactly the same thing, so in the past I've spent Christmas Eve in a bar, which is desperate and pathetic in its own way."

"I usually plan a trip somewhere tropical." She shrugged. "It sort of works."

He had a sudden image of Lacey in a bikini sipping an umbrella drink. He shoved that image away immediately. "That's classier than my option."

"Last Christmas I talked Lenny into flying to Bermuda, but he hated the fact it didn't feel like Christmas. I still wasn't ready for spending the holiday at his family's house or mine, so this was the compromise option."

Tucker blew out a breath. "I'm sorry it all fell apart, Lacey. He's an impatient creep who doesn't know what he's lost."

"To be honest, I was having doubts about the relationship. We weren't clicking the way I thought a committed couple should. Spending Christmas here was going to be a kind of test." She grimaced. "Guess it was, at that."

"You're way better off. You deserve somebody special." Any guy who rejected such a wonderful woman was terminally stupid.

"Thanks." Once again her eyes took on a happy gleam.

He hoped his next suggestion wouldn't bring back the shadows that had lurked in her gaze earlier. He cleared his throat. "Anyway, we're stuck together for at least tonight, and we understand each other's take on Christmas. I'm thinking it's the perfect chance to get over ourselves and celebrate the damned holiday."

3

"Celebrate Christmas?" Lacey couldn't believe he'd said that. Of all the people in the world, Tucker seemed the least likely to suggest such a thing. "We can't."

"Why not?"

"I didn't bring any decorations, for one thing. I had planned to, but when Lenny finked out, I donated all the stuff I'd bought to the Salvation Army."

"Except the soap."

She rolled her eyes. "Ah, yes, the soap. It was from a Secret Santa thing at work. I happened to be out of soap, so I brought it on this trip instead of throwing it in the Salvation Army donation bag. Are you suggesting we prop the soap on the mantel and call it good?"

He grinned at her. "It's a start."

That grin was lethal. She didn't really want to decorate for Christmas, but if he did, she was willing to go along just on the basis of that killer smile. He also had a point about celebrating with someone who understood the issues. She wouldn't have to fake anything with Tucker.

"I have some emergency candles in case the power goes out," she said. "We could put one on each side of the soap."

He nodded. "See how this plan is taking shape already?"

"Oh, yeah. We'll rival Rockefeller Center in no time."

"Don't make fun. Santa soap and candles could look really nice on the mantel, even if the candles aren't beeswax, which I'm guessing they're not."

"Nope. Just those cheap white paraffin kind." She gazed at him, marveling that he'd remembered a detail like beeswax candles. "So you really were listening when we had that conversation."

"Of course. Got any popcorn?"

"A couple of bags of the microwave kind, but—"

"Needle and thread?"

"Some. I carry a little sewing kit in my cosmetic bag, but—"

He pushed back his chair. "Then let's get popping. It needs to cool before we string it."

"Tucker, we don't have a tree."

"Don't worry." His green gaze found hers. "We will." Then he walked over and took his coat and hat off the peg where they were hanging by the front door.

"Wait a minute." She stood and followed him. "You can't go out there and cut down a tree. I'm renting this place. The landlord would have a fit."

"I'm not going to cut it down." He settled his hat on his head. "I'll dig it up. Then we can put it back in the ground later. No one has to know."

"The ground's frozen."

"Most places, yes, but on the sunny side of the cabin, it might not be as hard." He shoved his arms into the sleeves of his sheepskin coat.

"But there's a blizzard going on!" As if to emphasize the fact, the wind howled down the chimney and made the fire gyrate wildly.

"That makes it more exciting." He dazzled her with another smile. That combined with the shadow of a beard made him look rakish and slightly dangerous.

"You're crazy." Breathing quickly, both from the zing of attraction and her determination to stop him, she backed against the door, arms spread. "I won't let you go out there."

He winked, the picture of male assurance. "Yeah, you will. We're going to do this."

"No, we aren't. People get lost and die in snowstorms, sometimes when they're within a few feet of shelter because they get lost in all that whiteness."

He buttoned up his coat. "I know that. I promise to stay close enough to the cabin and the outbuilding that I can still see them."

"You could get distracted looking for a tree to dig up."

"I could, but I won't. By the way, do you have a shovel in your Jeep?"

"I'm not going to tell you."

"Which means yes."

"Doesn't matter." She remained planted firmly in front of the door. "I'm not moving."

His gaze reflected amusement as it swept over her. "I should warn you that once I get an idea in my head, I can't let it go."

"You'll have to let this one go." She lifted her chin in defiance. "I've been involved in too many search and rescue missions to allow you to take the chance of freezing to death out there. I'd given you more credit for good sense."

"There's your first mistake." And without warning, he leaned in and kissed her.

Her gasp of surprise allowed him to deepen the kiss, which quickly evolved into something spectacular. Bracing both hands against the door beside her head, he angled his mouth over hers and pressed in deep. The sweet invasion made her forget whatever silly argument they'd been having.

As his lips moved against hers in slow seduction, as his tongue explored with lazy intent, her senses rocketed back to the night of the Christmas formal. Yes, this was how she remembered his kiss — a take-no-prisoners assault that reduced her to a ragdoll willing to surrender to whatever he wanted.

She clutched his shoulders as the room seemed to spin. When he lifted his head to smile down at her, she realized the room hadn't been spinning, but she had. He'd circled her waist with both hands and turned her around so that she no longer blocked the door. She'd been so immersed in his kiss that she hadn't noticed.

"I promise not to get lost in the snow," he said. Then he released her and was out the door before she could frame a response.

"You don't fight fair!" she called after him when she managed to catch her breath.

The door opened a crack. "Nuke the popcorn!" Then he closed the door and was gone.

Grabbing the doorknob, she pulled the door open. A blast of frigid air filled with wet snow hit her in the face. "Use the rope!" She hurled the command out into the bitter cold where she could barely see him, head down, burrowing into the storm like a linebacker. "There's a long rope in the Jeep!"

"Thanks!" His answer was faint, but at least he'd heard and acknowledged her order.

She closed the door and stood there shivering, her arms wrapped protectively around her body. He was nuts, crazy as a loon. What kind of man risked his safety to bring a Christmas tree to a woman who didn't want to celebrate in the first place?

Yet she sensed that this wasn't all about her. In helping to slay her demons, he was also facing down his own. She couldn't very well deny him the chance to do that, and if he used the rope, tying it to the latch on the outbuilding and then around his waist, he would have a lifeline back to safety.

The rope was part of her search and rescue gear, but it would serve the purpose of orienting Tucker while he tried to locate a tree. People who lived in this part of the country often tied rope lines between the house and the barn so they'd have something to guide them when they checked on the animals during a snowstorm. Knowing Tucker would use that rope made her feel marginally better about him taking on this job.

He'd been a reckless kid in high school, and so far he'd confirmed that he still possessed that trait. Taking a snowmobile into the teeth of a storm to chase a runaway horse might be brave, but it was also foolish. If the horse had run in a different direction, away from all habitation... She didn't like to think how that might have turned out.

And yet... his reckless nature was part of what made him so sexy. When he'd impulsively kissed her, mostly to get his own way about the tree, she'd tasted a kind of thrilling abandon that didn't come her way often. In fact, she hadn't encountered it since the night of the Christmas formal.

Was that kiss simply a means to an end, getting past her objections to his plan? Or would he take it a step further when he returned? Then again, maybe he'd wait for her to make the next move.

Now that he was outside, she had a chance to think more clearly about what might or might not happen between them tonight. She should decide what she wanted now instead of making that decision in the heat of the moment. As she'd just discovered, a moment with Tucker could get very hot very fast.

Oh, who was she kidding? There was no decision to be made, here. Her fantasy man had appeared on her doorstep when neither of them was committed to someone else. If she ever intended to find out what making love to Tucker was all about, now was the time.

And that prospect set her panties on fire. She hurried into the bathroom and rummaged through her cosmetic case to see if... yes! By some fluke, she still had the box of condoms she'd become accustomed to taking along on trips with Lenny. He never seemed to remember, which should have been another sign that he was the wrong guy. The right guy wouldn't leave that responsibility up to the woman in his life.

She tucked the box back in the case and closed the lid. Her heart was beating so fast she pressed a hand to her chest and took a shaky breath. She had the man, and she had the condoms. This could be the best Christmas Eve of her entire life.

* * *

As needles of snow hit his cheeks and the wind threatened to blow him over on his way to the outbuilding, Tucker considered the fact that Lacey might be right. He very well could be crazy for coming out here to dig up a tree. Back in the cabin he'd pictured himself as a valiant hero who braved the storm to bring her an evergreen on Christmas Eve.

But when a guy made a boast like that, he had to come through or come off as a braggart who couldn't follow through. The possibility of staggering back into the cabin, treeless and frozen, hadn't occurred to him when he'd left. It sure as hell occurred to him now that he was in a pitched battle with the wind and the snow.

Adding to his idiocy was his most recent move — kissing Lacey. He really shouldn't have done that, but kissing her had seemed like a better option than standing there arguing with her. He'd known it would work to distract her.

Maybe, somewhere in his pea brain, he'd hoped she wouldn't kiss the way he remembered, which would help him put the brakes on his lust. But no. If anything, his memory hadn't done justice to the experience of going mouth-to-mouth with Lacey.

He thought again of Lenny and couldn't imagine how anyone could give up kisses like that. Maybe she didn't kiss Lenny the same way. Maybe Tucker brought out her inner wild woman.

Yeah, right. That kind of thinking was exactly what got him into trouble every damned time. He'd decide that the woman in question had never had someone love her right, and it was up to him, Supercock, to give her the kind of pleasure she deserved. He needed to forget that crap.

At the moment, he had one heroic job, and that involved digging up a Christmas tree. That should cool his jets for the time being. The storm was a humdinger.

Luckily he was moving into the wind, which pushed his hat onto his head. But on the way back he'd be in danger of losing it, especially if and when he dug up a tree and had to wrangle that back to the cabin. He was definitely nuts for doing this.

Well, maybe not entirely. He and Lacey really did need to get over their holiday issues. Speaking for himself, the idea of making Christmas happen for the first time since his mom died held a certain appeal. He'd never been moved to do it for anyone else, but he was obviously a sucker for Lacey. Sharing a

Christmas celebration with her seemed like the right thing to do on many counts.

But first he had to come up with the tree. And get into the damned outbuilding when snow had piled up against a door that was probably frozen shut by now. He kicked most of the snow away and pried open the latch.

This had sounded so easy when he'd described it to Lacey. Putting his whole weight behind the effort, he finally wrenched open the door with a loud crack. Instantly he positioned himself in the opening in case Houdini stood right there, ready to make a run for it. When no Houdini nose shoved against his chest, he slipped quickly inside and reached for the light switch as he pulled the door closed.

Houdini dozed peacefully in his allotted space next to the Jeep. Apparently the horse had worn himself out running through the snow earlier. Bonus. The Jeep looked okay, but some fresh chew marks on a two-by-four stud were probably Houdini's handiwork. Tucker decided not to worry about that now. He'd assess the damage after the storm ended.

Relieved that Houdini seemed to be settled into his temporary quarters just fine, Tucker rummaged in the back of the Jeep and located both a shovel and the hefty coil of rope. He also needed something for the tree's root ball, but the only bucket turned out to be the one he'd used for Houdini's oats. He'd need that again.

On a shelf near the door, he found an empty burlap sack and took that, instead. The outbuilding felt cozy, but Tucker didn't linger. He had a tree to dig up.

Once he was back outside in the bone-chilling cold, he secured the outbuilding's double doors and tied one end of the rope to the latch. He wrapped the other end around his waist and knotted it, although his dexterity was hampered by the freezing temperature and the shovel and the sack he held.

Finally he was armed and ready to bag himself a tree. Failure was not an option.

He took a moment to orient himself and walked around to the back side of the cabin, which faced south and had the most likelihood of unfrozen ground. He trailed Lacey's rope behind him. Although he'd initially imagined hauling in a man-sized blue spruce, he'd scaled back his expectations to a child-sized pine. In some things, size mattered. In this case, it was the thought that counted.

But he didn't have a lot of choices. Exactly one tree grew next to the cabin in what might be unfrozen ground. The tree had a nice shape, but it stood at least seven feet tall. Tucker surveyed the situation, took note of the condition of his fingers, toes, and nose, and decided digging up this very tree was the best he could hope for.

Some time later — could have been thirty minutes, could have been an hour, could have been two hours — he enclosed the tree's roots in the burlap sack and half-carried, half-dragged the tree around to the front of the cabin and up the steps to the small porch. She'd better love it, that's all he could say. He would have thought all that effort would have warmed him up, but instead he was one gigantic icicle.

As if she'd been listening for his approach, she threw open the door. "At last! I was ready to send out the St. Bernard with a keg of whiskey!"

"Took longer than I thought."

Her attention strayed to the tree lying on the porch. "Oh, Tucker. It's perfect." She stepped back so he could wrestle the tree inside. "Plus it smells *wonderful.*"

He'd have to take her word for it. His nostrils were frozen shut. He'd been mouth-breathing for what seemed like hours.

"I cleared a place for it in the corner."

Branches scraped along the hardwood floor and he hoped the tree wasn't leaking sap. Then he realized that nothing would be leaking sap, including him, when the outside temperature was this cold. All gelatinous substances would be solids by now.

He'd dug up as much of the root system as he had the energy for. Consequently, the tree had a solid base of roots and soil inside the burlap. Once he tipped the tree upright, it stood straight and looked magnificent, exactly as he'd pictured it would.

"Tucker, that's amazing."

He glanced over and discovered her gratitude and awe was directed at him, not the tree. He'd impressed her, and suddenly the ordeal was worth every finger-numbing, toe-numbing second he'd endured.

Feeling like Paul Bunyan, he stood back and admired his work. "Now *that's* a Christmas tree."

"Yes, it most definitely is."

Next he tried to unbutton his coat, which was a chore because he couldn't feel his fingers and had forgotten he was still wearing gloves.

"Here, let me help you with that." Moving in front of him, she gently pulled off his gloves and dropped them to the floor.

His fingers began to tingle as the numbness disappeared. He flexed them and decided he'd been through worse.

Then she began unfastening the buttons on his coat, which were coated with snow.

He let his arms drop to his sides and watched her intently pursuing her goal. If he wasn't so damned cold, this would be erotic. Good thing he was frozen, because now that he'd brought home the trophy tree, he had the unwise urge to claim his reward.

Fortunately his penis wouldn't be up to claiming anything until he'd thawed out some. Even then, he had another sizable issue that would keep his bad boy in check. Thank God he was totally condomless. The heady feeling of being admired and fussed over for his tree-bagging abilities was making mincemeat of his vow not to get physical with her.

"You're really shaking, Tucker. I'm worried that you're suffering from mild hypothermia." She peeled off his coat and dropped it on the floor, too.

He doubted that. He'd been dealing with this kind of weather all his life, and he'd never had a problem with it. But he was human, and having her fret over his well-being felt nice, so he kept his mouth shut.

"Sit down on the couch. I'll take off your boots."

He complied.

She pulled off his boots with brisk efficiency and then removed his wool socks. "God, your feet are like ice."

He didn't know if they were or not. He couldn't feel them yet.

"Come with me." She grasped his hand, which was still prickling, and urged him to his feet. "What you need is to get out of these clothes and into a warm bed."

He couldn't recall ever refusing a beautiful woman's invitation to get into her bed, but he had to refuse this time. "That's okay. I'll be fine here by the fire."

"Look, this isn't up for debate. I'm not about to have you put your health at risk because of this daring tree project. It was a wonderful gesture, and I want you to be well enough to enjoy it." She tugged harder. "Now, come on. Don't make me get nasty."

He had to admit that crawling into a warm bed sounded terrific, at least until he warmed up. She hadn't said she'd get in there with him, so maybe it would be okay. Once he wasn't shivering so much, he'd get dressed again and they'd decorate the tree together.

"Okay. Just for a few minutes." He allowed himself to be led into the bedroom. Nothing would happen there. Without condoms, nothing *could* happen there. End of story.

_4_

Lacey wasn't about to let Tucker's heroic Christmas tree project put him at risk. The fact that he was still shaking was a good sign and meant his body was still trying to warm itself. But he'd been out there nearly an hour, and she wasn't taking any chances considering how isolated they were.

She'd put him to bed and brew him some tea. Anyone who'd dealt with hypothermia would do the same. The fact that he was six-foot-plus of dark-haired, green-eyed yumminess wasn't the dominant factor, here.

But it was a factor. She threw back the covers on the cabin's queen-sized bed before turning to him. Her gaze traveled from his broad shoulders to his narrow hips, and she swallowed. Taking off his gloves and coat were one thing. Removing the rest of his clothes was quite another.

She glanced into his eyes, which seemed somewhat unfocused. "Do you think you can undress yourself?"

His teeth chattered as he continued to shiver. "Sure. Go on back by the f-fire. I'll b-be fine." He fumbled with the snaps on his shirt.

"Never mind." She nudged his hands away. "It'll go faster if I do it." Taking a deep breath, she tackled the snaps. The material was cold, but she was encouraged by the warmth of his body underneath. He was still quivering, but at least his skin wasn't clammy. "I think you're going to be okay. This is just a precaution."

He nodded as he stood meekly letting her unfasten the snaps at his wrists and pull the shirt from his waistband. Once she'd tossed the shirt on the floor, she worked his T-shirt off. He leaned down slightly so she could pull it over his head.

At that point her objectivity began to slip. She forced herself to ignore the breadth of his chest, the dark hair sprinkled over it, and the intoxicating scent of his skin. She reminded herself that hypothermia was serious, a condition not to be messed with.

Keeping that thought foremost in her mind, she reached for his belt buckle. But as she did, his hand closed over hers.

"That's good enough," he said. "You can stop, now."

She glanced up and met a gaze so hot she nearly went up in flames.

"I don't need to crawl into that bed, after all." His voice was husky. "If you'll just go on out to the living room and wait for me, I'll be there in a few minutes."

Her heart raced and moisture gathered between her thighs. It didn't take a genius to figure out that she'd aroused him with the undressing routine. Standing here by the bed presented the ideal opportunity to do something about that. She admitted the possibility of sex with him had been in the back of her mind, assuming he really didn't have hypothermia.

And yet Tucker acted as if he didn't intend to take advantage of the situation she'd created for them. Given his reputation and his obvious attraction to her, she had to believe he wanted to. Lack of birth control had to be the thing stopping him.

So now what? Should she announce that she had a box of condoms? That seemed sort of… tacky. But if she didn't let him know about them, he would continue to avoid any possibility of having sex with her tonight. That would be a waste for both of them.

"I mean it, Lacey. You need to leave."

She kept looking into his eyes because they were begging her to stay even though his words told her to go. She swallowed. "What… what if I don't want to leave?"

He groaned. "It's best if you do."

"What would you say if I told you I have… condoms?"

His eyes widened.

"I was always in charge of bringing them, and I forgot to take them out of my travel case for this trip."

"You were always in charge of condoms? What kind of man expects that of a woman?"

"The same kind who dumps her right before Christmas, I guess. Anyway, I have them."

He blew out a breath. "Right."

Oh, God. The issue wasn't condoms. Or if it was, he was put off by the idea of using some bought for another man. What she'd thought was a happy accident might be a colossal insult.

How awkward was this? Her face hot with embarrassment, she looked away. "Never mind," she murmured. "Forget I said anything. I'll see you in the living room." She started to leave.

"Wait." He caught her arm.

"Listen, Tucker, I'm sure your instincts are on target." She still didn't look at him.

"Or maybe yours are." He pulled her gently back until she was facing him. "Just so you know, I want you desperately."

"Yes, but you have misgivings."

His smile was soft. "Not anymore." And then he kissed her with such thoroughness that she believed him.

He continued to kiss her until her resistance disappeared and her body grew molten with desire. Soon nothing was more important than making love with Tucker. And even though he had a reputation for making any woman he touched feel that way, she knew that for this moment, she was the only one who mattered to him. That was enough.

At last he released her and brushed his thumb slowly over her well-kissed mouth. "The condoms are where?"

"Finish getting out of your clothes." She moved reluctantly from the warmth of his arms and headed for the door. "I'll get the box."

Once she was in the bathroom, she told herself not to look in the mirror, but of course she did, and groaned in dismay. Hair going every which way, no makeup, and worst of all, her pink cheeks and sparkling eyes made her look *wholesome*. Tucker had never dated wholesome girls in high school, and she'd bet good money he didn't date wholesome girls now, either.

But then she remembered the way he'd kissed her just now, and there was nothing wholesome about the way she'd kissed him back. She wasn't the shy virgin he'd met outside the school gym that night. She shouldn't be worrying about whether she'd measure up to the other women he'd had.

"Lacey?" he called out from the bedroom. "Is everything okay?"

"Yes," she called back. Grabbing the box of condoms, she walked across the hall and into the bedroom.

Tucker sat up in bed, the covers pulled to his waist. He was leaning casually against a pillow he'd placed between his back and the headboard, but there was nothing casual about the way he looked at her. His gaze was intense, and the hint of a frown creased the spot between his dark eyebrows.

He took a deep breath, and his magnificent chest heaved. "I wondered if you'd changed your mind."

"I haven't changed my mind, but... I'll admit to being a little intimidated by you."

His frown deepened. "Intimidated?"

"You had quite a reputation in high school."

He grimaced. "Don't believe everything you hear."

"Even if I didn't believe all of it, I'm pretty sure that you're more skilled and experienced at this than I am. So..." She paused, her pulse racing out of control. "What if I'm a big disappointment?"

He met her gaze. "I guess it's always possible."

"You think so?" She really hadn't expected him to agree with her. Most men she knew, when presented with a willing woman holding a box of condoms, would brush aside any concerns and get to the action.

"But then, I could be a big disappointment to you, too."

"I seriously doubt that, Tucker."

"After listening to all the gossip, you're probably expecting me to be the best you've ever had."

She couldn't deny it, so she said nothing.

"That's a lot of pressure."

She felt ashamed of herself. "You're right. I'm sorry, Tucker. I didn't really think about—"

"On the other hand, it's possible I will be the best you've ever had." His wicked grin flashed. "Why don't you take off those clothes so you can find out?"

She nearly passed out from excitement. She couldn't breathe from the force of it. Now that was the kind of comment she would have expected from him. Heart pounding wildly, she tossed him the box of condoms.

He caught them in one hand without taking his gaze from hers. "For all you know," he said quietly, "I'm expecting you to be the best I've ever had."

Her reply was breathless. "Please don't get your hopes up." With trembling hands, she started removing her clothes.

"Sex is like dancing." Still looking into her eyes, he opened the box of condoms, reached over and upended it on the nightstand. "You're only as good as your partner."

She'd never seen a man empty a box of condoms like that, as if he might need the entire contents eventually and wanted them all available. "That could work both ways," she said. "I could cramp your style." She'd peeled off everything but her bra and panties. If only they were black silk instead of white cotton.

"No, you won't."

She reached behind her back, unfastened her bra, and let it slide down her arms to the floor.

He groaned softly. "You *seriously* won't. Look at you."

Her body grew several degrees hotter. "I'm nothing special."

"That's where you're wrong. You're perfect."

No man had ever called her perfect before, and it must have gone to her head, because as she slipped off her panties, she added a little shimmy to the move.

"You're killing me, Lacey. I need you over here ASAP."

"You do?" She wasn't sure where the temptress voice had come from, either. "Why is that?"

He threw back the covers to reveal his gloriously erect penis. "Does that answer your question?"

She thought she could be forgiven for staring. A girl wasn't treated to something that beautiful every day. In fact, this particular girl had never seen equipment quite so gorgeous.

It summoned an ache from deep inside her, an ache demanding to be assuaged. For the first time in her life she understood the concept of penis envy. If she could have that particular penis available to her on a regular basis, she would be the envy of every woman in the state of Wyoming.

She sashayed slowly over to the bed. She'd never sashayed before, but she was inspired to do it now. "You need to put on its party outfit."

In one smooth movement, he picked up a condom packet from the nightstand and handed it to her. "You can do the honors."

"I'd be delighted." She quivered with eagerness, and even though she'd never been called upon to do this before, she vowed to be cool about it. She ripped open the package. "I've heard moistening it helps."

"It's already moist. And you won't like the taste."

"Oh, I bet I will." Heart hammering, she sat on the edge of the bed, wrapped her fingers around his penis, and lowered her mouth to the glistening tip.

"I meant the taste of the cond— ahhhh... never mind."

She raised her head. "Did I do something wrong?"

"Nope." His eyes had glazed over. "That's great. More of that."

"Okay." Sucking gently, she took him in all the way to the back of her throat and heard him mutter a soft curse. She lifted her head again. "Problem?"

"Uh-huh." His voice sounded strained. "You're very good."

"And that's bad?" He was so velvety soft, yet so deliciously firm that she couldn't resist stroking him.

"It can be." His jaw tightened. "If you keep that up, the party will be over before you know it."

She stopped stroking immediately. "I don't want that."

"Neither do I."

"I thought, with all your experience, you'd be able to—"

"You'd think so, wouldn't you? But watching that curly mop of yours sliding up and down while you — I can't take it."

She touched her hair, suddenly self-conscious. "I know my hair's a mess."

"A wonderful mess." He shoved his fingers into her hair and cradled her head in both hands. "Your hair is perfect for making love all night long." Then he kissed her with such enthusiasm that she forgot all about the state of her hair.

She had to believe that she was perfect, and her hair was perfect, and something about her was so potent that he lost all the sexual control he'd developed over the years. He finally stopped kissing her long enough for her to focus on putting the condom on.

Earlier he must have thought she was going to put the condom in her mouth before rolling it over his penis. She wouldn't have done that, but he'd given her another idea. She was moist in other places, too, and a devilish urge made her put the condom down there to gather up some extra lubrication.

He watched her in rapt fascination. "I'm in serious trouble with you, lady."

"Then let's get into trouble together." She rolled on the condom. By the time she'd finished, he was breathing like a long-distance runner nearing the finish line. "I'm usually a lot calmer about this, Lacey, but..."

"But I get you really, really, hot."

"That's an understatement. Crude as this might sound, you'd better climb on before the train leaves the station."

If she'd been expecting a long, slow seduction where he aroused her to a fever pitch by kissing her all over, she wasn't going to get it, at least not this time. Truthfully, long and slow would have frustrated the hell out of her. She'd gone way past simmer to a full boil, and she wanted him to do her *now*. He could take his sweet time later.

Bracing her hands on his shoulders, she straddled his hips.

"I love your breasts." He cupped them in his large hands. "I haven't paid enough attention to them."

"Don't worry about it." Centering herself over the object of her desire, she wiggled a little to make sure she had him where she wanted him.

He made a strangled sound deep in his throat and his fingers flexed, lightly squeezing her breasts. "Don't wait."

"I won't." And with that, she lowered herself with deliberation, taking him up to the hilt, closing her eyes and moaning as he stretched and filled her. Ecstasy.

He gulped for air and brushed his thumbs over her taut nipples. Tilting her head back, she reveled in the erotic friction and instinctively responded by starting to lift her hips in preparation for another downward stroke.

Suddenly his hands were there, gripping her tight, holding her down. "Be still for a second. Let me... get my bearings."

She opened her eyes and looked into his. The wild hunger she saw in those green depths made her womb contract.

He gasped. "Lacey..."

"Didn't mean to. I just—"

"I know. Me, too. We might have to go for it."

"I'm in."

His grip tightened on her hips as he held her gaze. "Then ride me, Lacey. Give me all you've got."

Clutching his shoulders and looking into his eyes, she rose up and came down, rose up again and came down faster.

"*Yeah.*" He urged her on, guiding the motion of her hips. "Like that. Like *that.*"

Her orgasm thundered closer with every wild thrust. Her bottom smacked against his thighs, and she began to utter little cries that grew louder, and louder yet. She realized that they were utterly and completely alone. No one could hear, and she could let go as she'd never let go before.

His jaw flexed. "Come for me, Lacey. Come for me!"

She couldn't have stopped her climax if she'd tried. It engulfed her, making her abandon all modesty as she pressed down on that glorious cock and arched into a mindless spiral of sensation. Holding her tight, he drove upward with a bellow of satisfaction, finding the open gate to nirvana and joining her there.

For those few moments, they seemed inseparable. She'd never felt that intensity of emotion, that unique oneness with anyone else. She'd expected polished technique from a man like Tucker. She'd expected pleasure and sinful delight. But she'd never, in her wildest dreams, expected... transcendence.

She wanted to believe she was special, and that the connection had been as unique for him as it had been for her. But that was probably a foolish hope. He was an accomplished lover, the kind of guy who could have almost any woman he wanted.

In a twist of Fate, a blizzard had trapped him with her for the night. He'd gallantly made her feel like the only woman in the world for him. He probably did that no matter who he took to bed, and she'd do well to remember that.

5

Tucker realized soon after the most profound climax of his life that he was screwed. He'd allowed his hero complex to take over again, and he would pay dearly for that. But hell, she'd been almost engaged to a guy that made *her* buy the condoms?

That had been bad enough, but when he saw the look on her face when she'd thought he was rejecting her hesitant offer to have sex, he hadn't been able to stand it. She deserved so much more than the jerk she'd been going with. Tucker didn't consider himself in the *so much more* category, but he could at least make her feel good on Christmas Eve.

Well, now, he had. From her wild response and the way her body had clenched his during her orgasm, he was certain he'd given her a happy time. And because no good deed went unpunished, he'd just had the most soul-shattering sexual experience of his life.

If history repeated itself, and it usually did, Lacey would either move on or go back to her ex. Either way he was hosed, and this time he wasn't sure how well he'd handle it. True, the rebound guy didn't always get kicked to the curb. He shouldn't automatically assume that Lacey would do that.

He'd love some reassurance that she wouldn't, but how did you ask a woman if she'd felt reality shift in the last few minutes? For all he knew, she always responded with that kind of enthusiasm. He rather doubted it, but trying to find out would be awkward, to say the least. He'd sound like a loser lacking all self-confidence.

She slumped against him, her forehead resting on his shoulder, her breathing slowly returning to normal.

He rubbed her back, marveling at the silky texture of her skin. He'd always imagined that she'd feel like this, but imagining and knowing were such different things. Now he'd never forget the softness under his fingertips. And he'd want to experience it again and again. That might not be in the cards for him.

As he thought about that, he decided on his plan of action. He'd suggested that they celebrate Christmas with a tree, candles, a popcorn garland, and a bar of Santa soap. They should follow through on that, and maybe when they weren't in this bed, he'd get an inkling of her true attitude toward him and toward a potential continuation of this relationship.

For years he'd regretted not following up on that kiss. He'd sometimes thought that she couldn't possibly be as perfect for him as he'd imagined. As it turned out, she was even more perfect.

He finger-combed her butterscotch curls. "If we don't get that tree decorated soon, Santa won't leave you any presents."

She stirred and lifted her head to smile lazily at him. "Who needs presents?"

He considered that a promising statement. "Good point, but after all I went through to bring a tree inside, I think we should put some kind of decorations on it."

She laughed softly. "Nag, nag, nag."

"Did you nuke the popcorn?"

"I did."

"Then let's go string it."

She gazed into his eyes. "You're really serious about this, aren't you?"

"Crazy as it seems, I am. This is the most traction I've ever gotten on the Christmas thing since my mom passed away. I feel a breakthrough coming on."

She nodded. "Then we should honor that."

"Thank you." He was reminded that she was a truly nice person who, if she let him down, would let him down easy.

About twenty minutes later, they'd dressed and laid out their supplies on the kitchen table. She'd volunteered to string popcorn, and he was making a chain of aluminum foil, twisting the foil into links. In his opinion it was an improvement over construction paper and paste, which he didn't have on hand, anyway.

She poked a sewing needle carefully through a piece of popcorn, her head bent and her expression focused. "I'd forgotten how much I like doing this."

He thought about mentioning that she looked adorable stringing popcorn, her rosy lips pursed and her brow puckered in concentration. He decided against saying anything. Too many comments like that and he might scare her off.

Glancing up, she noticed his chain. "That's awesome. I never would have thought of that, but it'll reflect the light."

"We used to cut strips of foil and hang it as icicles, but this is better."

"We need something to give the tree a little color, though." Lost in thought, she continued to string popcorn. Then she glanced up, her eyes alight. "Hershey's kisses! I just remembered I have a bag of them I brought for snacks. Naturally this time of year they're wrapped in red, green and silver. We can tie threads on them and hang them from the branches!"

"Ingenious." She didn't need Hershey's kisses when he was prepared to shower her with the real kind. In fact, he already missed touching her, and they'd only been working on this project for ten minutes. At least they'd agreed to only decorate the front of the tree.

A foil chain could be created much faster than a popcorn garland, and soon he had one about twelve feet long. Standing, he draped it on the tree in a zig-zag pattern.

"Very pretty." Her eyes sparkled in that happy way that made his heart swell with satisfaction. "I'm going to remember that trick," she said. "It's really effective."

"Are you saying you might decorate a tree again next year?" God, he wanted to be there if she did.

Her smile dimmed a little. "I don't know."

"I'd help you." He held his breath.

"That would be nice. I mean, if you're available."

"It shouldn't be a problem." He could tell she was hedging her bets, but then, so was he. She hadn't rejected his offer to help her with a tree next year.

He'd take that as a reasonable beginning. "I'll start on the kisses if you want."

She lifted her face to his, her lips curved in a tempting smile. "Which kind?"

Lust slammed into him, but he held himself in check, not wanting her to know just how much he craved her. Not yet, anyway. Bracing his hands on the table, he leaned in close. "You tell me."

Heat smoldered in her eyes, but then she grinned. "Hershey's, I guess. If you start on the other kind, we'll never finish decorating this tree, and you did haul it in here at great personal sacrifice."

"Now that you mention it, shouldn't you give me at least one kiss in honor of that great personal sacrifice?"

"All right. Just one." She closed her eyes.

He could have moved a few inches and touched his lips to hers, but he didn't.

She opened her eyes again. "I thought you wanted a kiss?"

"I do. I thought you were going to give me one."

"I am. Go ahead."

"Nope. This is my reward, which means you're supposed to kiss *me*."

"Oh. I see the distinction." Putting down her popcorn garland, she reached up with both hands, took him by the ears, and pulled him forcefully down to connect with her laughing mouth.

He was laughing, too, but about three seconds into the kiss, the mood shifted. With a soft moan, she let go of his ears, tunneled her fingers through his hair and thrust her tongue in deep. Desperate to feel her against him, he dragged her out of the chair and heard it clatter to the floor.

No matter. Keeping his mouth firmly on hers, he scooped her up, kicked the chair out of the way, and carried her into the bedroom. Laying her crossways on the bed, he followed her down as he fumbled with her clothes and she wrenched his shirt open, the snaps popping like gunfire.

He hadn't paid nearly enough attention to her breasts the first time, but he made up for it now. After he yanked her sweater over her head, she arched her back so he could unhook her bra. Soon that joined the sweater on the far side of the bed.

If he'd been hot before, the tactile pleasure of her breasts beneath his hands and mouth turned him into an inferno. He stroked, nipped, and tasted until he was wild from wanting her. But he couldn't have her until they'd both rid themselves of their jeans.

Gasping, he pushed himself away from her rosy nipples and stood at the side of the bed so he could shuck his pants. She took her cue from him and wiggled out of hers. That wiggle temporarily mesmerized him as a surge of desire took his breath away.

She wasn't practiced at being seductive, yet somehow she'd turned out to be the sexiest woman he'd ever taken to bed. Every move she made turned him on. He was fascinated by her.

Once she was naked, she scooted around so she was lying lengthwise on the bed. Then she reached for one of the packets on the nightstand, and he realized he was just standing there gaping at her when he should be moving this process along.

Taking the packet from her outstretched hand, he put on the condom. If he only had this glorious opportunity to be with her for one night, he was still one lucky cowboy, and he needed to let her know that.

He could do it by slowing the pace and loving her the way she deserved to be loved, instead of behaving like a rutting bull elk. He moved over her carefully, dropping soft kisses on her cheeks, her eyelids, and finally, on her mouth. "Thank you," he murmured.

Breathing fast, she slid her hands up his chest. "For the condom?"

"That, too." He nuzzled the tender spot behind her ear. "But mostly for allowing me to stay with you tonight."

"I couldn't very well let you freeze to death." Her hands roamed around to his back, stroking, kneading, caressing.

"No, but you didn't have to let me do this." He ran his tongue along her collarbone and felt her shiver beneath him. "Or this." Leaning down, he placed a ring of kisses around her nipple.

"Which I hope is leading to this." She grasped his cock and gave it a quick squeeze.

"Lacey!" Lifting his head, he looked into eyes bright with a combination of lust and laughter. "Damn it, I'm trying to be romantic."

She resumed massaging his chest. "I appreciate that, Tucker, but you had the RPMs way up there a few seconds ago, and as a consequence I'm still operating full throttle. How about you drop the clutch and peel out?"

"But I want you to know that I cherish this—"

"I know you do. You nearly froze to death digging up a Christmas tree so I could have a real one to decorate. Then you carried me into the bedroom. No man's ever done that, bodily picked me up and taken me to bed."

"They haven't?" He felt good about that.

"Nope. And let me tell you, it makes a girl feel special to be carried into the bedroom like Scarlett O'Hara."

"Good. I want you to feel special."

"You know what else makes a girl feel special?"

"What?"

"When a guy is so desperate to have her, he can't wait another second. She can see that he has this intense need to thrust deep inside her, to join with her in the most basic way that a man and a woman—"

"Got it." Holding her gaze, he drew back and swiftly buried his cock up to the hilt. The sensation of being inside her while he looked into her eyes made him dizzy with joy. He took a shaky breath. "Like that?"

"Exactly like that." Her blue eyes seemed to mirror the intensity he felt. As she cupped his face in both hands, her words came out in a breathless rush. "If you ask me, this is pretty romantic."

"Glad you think so." He drew back and rocked forward again, moving in tight, locking them together. "How about that?"

"Even more romantic."

"Then lady, get ready to be romanced out of your mind." He began a steady, insistent rhythm, thrusting deep each time. He felt triumphant as her eyes darkened and her skin flushed pink. Her hands fluttered from his face to his shoulders, and then to his hips. Her fingers dug in as she rose to meet him and began to whimper with need.

As her cries increased in urgency, he bore down, seeking her climax, but also seeking something more, something elusive. He longed to reach the essence of her, to touch that part of her that no other man had ever touched.

Her body moved in perfect time with his as they joined in a race to ecstasy. And then, as if she'd flung open a door, he felt it — her complete and utter surrender. He abandoned the last of his restraint, giving to her as she'd given to him, holding nothing back, driving into her again and again, his cries echoing hers.

Her spasms began a breath before his, and he shouted with the joy of it as they came and came and came... together.

For long moments his body shook as he stayed braced above her. He'd closed his eyes at the very last, the better to focus on the rolling splendor of climaxing when she did. But now he opened his eyes and looked down at her.

She gasped for breath, obviously unable to speak yet. But her luminous gaze told him more than words that he hadn't been wrong. Something magical had happened between them.

As her breathing slowed, she reached up and stroked his cheek. "I love how you make me feel," she murmured.

"That's good." He cleared sudden emotion from his throat. "Because I love how you make me feel, too." He had no idea if this magic between them would last for an hour or a lifetime, but he vowed to be grateful for the gift and not worry about its duration.

He leaned down and kissed her. "Come on," he murmured. "We need to finish decorating the tree."

"You're a tough task master."

He lifted his head to smile at her. "You know you want to."

"I do, actually. I want to see how that popcorn garland looks once it's done."

"See, I knew it. Besides, I think we have a good system going."

"Oh? What's that?"

"Make love, decorate the tree, make love, decorate the tree." He punctuated his sentence with more kisses. "That's working for me."

"Yeah, but eventually we'll have the tree all decorated. Then what?"

He gave her a stricken look. "I guess we'll just have to make love nonstop after that."

"Wow, that sounds drastic."

"I know." He shrugged. "But that's all we'll have left. We'll have to make the best of it."

_6_

The system worked to perfection, and as Lacey had predicted, they ran out of decorations and ended up back in bed for the rest of the night. Eventually they even went to sleep in that bed, with Lacey nestled inside the curve of Tucker's body.

She woke up in the gray light of dawn with a sense of safety, peace, and happiness she hadn't felt in years. Tucker was already up, and the sound of a crackling fire and the scent of evergreen and coffee brewing filled her with memories of waking up as a child on Christmas morning.

Throwing back the covers she shivered in the chilly bedroom as she pulled her blue terry bathrobe and fuzzy blue slippers out of the closet. Of course there would be no presents under the tree, but anticipation bubbled through her anyway. It was Christmas morning and she had someone special to spend it with.

He sat on the couch in front of the fire drinking a mug of coffee, but he put the mug on the end table immediately and stood when she came in the room. His smile flashed. "Merry Christmas."

He'd lit the emergency candles sitting on the mantel, and light from the fire reflected off the aluminum foil chain and Hershey's kisses. Her snowy white popcorn garland was the perfect touch against the dark green branches. As if that weren't enough, a foil-wrapped box lay at the base of the tree. It even had a fluffy white bow.

She glanced at Tucker. "A present?"

"It's not much."

She approached the tree, marveling at how he could have come up with anything at all under the circumstances. No matter what he'd put in that box, she was touched to the point of feeling her throat close up. It was Christmas morning, and a wonderful man had somehow created a present for her to open.

Sitting on the floor beside the tree, exactly as she used to when she was little, she picked up the box, her eyes moist. Then she laughed softly. The ribbon was toilet paper.

She cleared her throat. "You're very clever."

"I used more than I wanted to, because it kept tearing."

"You did all this while I was asleep?"

He nodded and walked over, mug in hand. "It's funny, but I never used to be able to sleep on Christmas Eve. I was always too excited. It's like that feeling sort of came back."

She gazed up at him. "I know what you mean. When I woke up and smelled the tree and heard the fire, it made me all cozy and warm inside, like I used to feel on Christmas morning. Then I walked in here and discovered a present." She patted the floor beside her. "Come and sit with me while I open it."

"Okay, but I hope you're not expecting too much." He leaned down and set his coffee mug on the floor before sitting cross-legged beside her.

"The fact that this present even exists is a miracle. I didn't think about dreaming up a gift for you."

He shrugged. "Like I said, I was too excited to sleep."

"Well, I'm very impressed that you did this." She tried to get the bow off without tearing it, but it came apart despite her careful effort. "Sorry."

"Hey, it's just toilet paper. Don't worry about it."

"Yes but you worked so hard to make the bow. I wanted to save it." She tucked the wad of toilet paper in her bathrobe pocket and took off the aluminum foil wrapper. Underneath was a box of graham crackers, except it felt too light to still have crackers in it.

"I put the packets of crackers in the cupboard so I could use the box."

"I am just amazed at your ingenuity."

He leaned closer. "Be careful when you open it."

"It's not alive, is it?"

"No, but it's kind of delicate."

She glanced over at him and her heart squeezed. He'd made her something and now he was almost breathless as he waited to find out what she thought of it. Her world shifted in that moment as she fell helplessly, hopelessly in love.

Opening the top of the cracker box, she reached gently inside and pulled out... a foil angel.

"It's for the top of the tree," he said.

"It's beautiful."

"Hey, are you crying?"

"No." She sniffed and wiped her eyes. "Yes. Oh, Tucker." Laying the angel carefully on the floor next to the tree, she turned to him and climbed into his lap.

He wrapped his arms around her and held her close. "I didn't mean to make you cry."

"They're good tears." She nestled against his warm body and sighed. "It feels like Christmas."

"Yes." He stroked her hair. "Yes, it does."

* * *

The morning felt so right that Tucker hated to think about leaving. But the storm had ended and he needed to contact the ranch. After attaching the angel to the top of the tree, he shoveled a path to the outbuilding and gave Houdini the rest of the oats and some of the carrots Lacey had left over. Then he texted Jack, who responded that someone would be over with a snowmobile within the next two hours.

Tucker relayed that information to Lacey over breakfast. She'd served him scrambled eggs, bacon, and the best cinnamon toast he'd ever eaten. He wanted to stay and spend the day with her, but that wouldn't be happening for several reasons.

First of all, he had to help get Houdini back home. And although Lacey was on vacation, he wasn't. The ranch was short-staffed over the holidays, and he was needed there. He'd made a point of saying he would cover for the hands who'd gone home to their families over Christmas.

He gazed at her sitting across the table from him. She still wore her bathrobe. Without makeup and with her hair still tousled, she looked like a teenager. He thought how wonderful life would be if he could spend every morning across the breakfast table with her.

He put down his coffee mug with a sigh. "I hate to go."

"Couldn't you come back later? Borrow a different snowmobile?"

He shook his head. "Not really. They need me at the ranch." Then he had an idea. "Would you like to come over there for Christmas dinner? I'm sure they'll want to show their appreciation for what you've done, and at least that way we could spend some time together."

She regarded him steadily. "I would love that."

"Great! Dinner's around four. I'll come over with a snowmobile and get you about three, and then bring you back here after dinner. I won't be able to stay all night, but I could stay for... a little while."

"Okay." Her smile told him she knew exactly how they'd spend that *little while*. "That sounds very nice."

It sounded more than nice to him. It sounded promising.

"And by the way, I'm looking forward to seeing all the decorations at the ranch." She swept a hand around the room. "All this has changed my attitude. You were smart to insist on creating our own celebration."

"It worked for me, too. I—" He heard a cell phone, but it wasn't his. "I think you have a call."

"Yeah." She looked disconcerted. "Excuse me." She picked up her phone from the kitchen counter and walked into the bedroom with it.

Tucker wasn't sure how he knew who had called, but he knew, all the same. He'd bet his last dollar Lenny was on the phone. His stomach felt queasy and he stood up, unable to sit any longer. Coffee mug in hand, he paced the living room.

He couldn't hear what Lacey said, but from the low pitch of her voice, he knew the conversation was serious. Maybe something had come up regarding a member of her family. He tried to convince himself this was a family matter, but he didn't believe it. The way things worked in his world, the minute he started getting invested in a woman, something like this happened.

After what seemed like an eternity, she walked out of the bedroom. "That was Lenny."

His stomach pitched. "Oh?"

"He misses me." She looked slightly dazed. "He said he made a terrible mistake by breaking up with me and he wants to get back together. He said he'd find a way to get out here today, so we could spend the holiday the way we'd planned."

He wanted to yell at her that Lenny couldn't come to this cabin and enjoy the tree he'd dug up, or the decorations he'd made, or the woman he'd fallen in love with. Because he was in love with Lacey, probably had been a little bit in love with her for years.

Cruelly, he'd had these few hours to fall completely head-over-heels, and now she would go back to Lenny because that's what women did. They had a great time with Tucker and then went back to their regularly scheduled lives.

He swallowed. "So I guess you won't be coming over to the Last Chance, after all."

"I didn't say that." There was an edge to her voice.

He started the painful process of putting blockades around his heart. "No, but you won't, will you?"

"I don't know, Tucker." She sounded almost angry. "Do you want me to?"

"That's entirely up to you, Lacey." He might have said more, but the roar of a snowmobile cut off their conversation. It was too soon for Lenny to be arriving, so it had to be someone from the Last Chance. Tucker grabbed his hat and coat from the peg by the door. "I need to get going."

"I'm sure you do."

He paused by the door. "Give the ranch a call if you decide you want to come for dinner." He'd deliberately said the ranch because he'd never given her his cell phone number and he wasn't going to stop and do it now. He had to get the hell out of there before the pain overwhelmed him. She was going back to Lenny. Goddammit, she was going back to that idiot Lenny!

* * *

Lacey stood without moving, her cell phone clutched in her hand. Tucker hadn't been able to get out of here fast enough, and her head was still spinning from his dash to freedom. She could hear him outside laughing and joking with whoever had come to pick him up. It seemed as if he'd already put her out of his mind.

Heartbreaking though it might be, she had to face the possibility that she was simply a bright spot in his life, a person he'd remember fondly but not someone he'd keep around for the long haul. Years ago Tucker had dated lots of girls, but he'd never stuck with one for very long. Maybe he was built that way.

When she'd told him about Lenny, he'd leaped to the conclusion that she was going back to him. Maybe he'd been relieved about that. He'd left the Christmas dinner invitation up to her instead of saying that he really wanted her there. In actuality, she had no idea how much she meant to Tucker. She only knew how much he meant to her.

He'd left before she could tell him what she'd said to Lenny. *What we had wasn't love. I know that, now, because I've truly fallen in love, maybe for the first time in my life.*

How odd that she'd told Lenny, but Tucker was oblivious. If she had any pride at all, he would remain oblivious. Then she looked at the tree in the corner with the angel on top and decided that pride was overrated.

Tucker might not know it, but he had a lot of love to give and she was just the person who could bring it out in him. She wasn't going to abandon her feelings for him because he was too dense to realize he needed her. They needed each other. They'd proved that last night and this morning.

Loving him seemed right, and even if he didn't totally love her back, he had some affection for her. After all, he'd dug up the tree for her, and he'd made an angel to go on top of it. Those two things meant more, in her estimation, than the great sex they'd shared, although that was a bonus. It was good to be turned on by the man you loved.

The sound of the snowmobile starting up prompted her to walk over to the window. They'd tied Houdini's lead rope to the back of the snowmobile and Tucker was just now climbing on behind whoever had driven over to get him. He turned and glanced back at the cabin.

She raised a hand in farewell, even though she didn't think he could see her. But she counted it as a good sign that he'd looked back. He might not be as ready to write her off as he'd seemed. She wondered if pride had kept him from telling her that she meant something to him.

Glancing at the cell phone in her hand, she took note of the time. She'd give him a couple of hours to get situated before she called and asked for a ride to the ranch. She had no intention of waiting until three.

She wasn't nearly through with him, and he wasn't through with her, either, not if she could help it. If nothing else, she could use some help replanting the tree he'd dug up.

* * *

Tucker was getting dressed after a long-overdue shave and shower when the bunkhouse phone rang. He was the only person down there, so he hurried over to the wall phone while he fastened the snaps on his dark green western shirt. He picked up the phone. "This is Tucker."

"Hey, Tuck." Jack's voice boomed over the phone and raucous noise in the background indicated the Christmas party was starting a little earlier than planned.

Tucker decided from Jack's cheerful tone that he was already into the eggnog. The guy had seemed damned happy to get Houdini back in one piece, and Tucker had now become Tuck, which he took as a sign of Jack's goodwill. "What's up?"

"That woman you stayed with last night called here asking if you'd come over and pick her up. She said you invited her for dinner. Did you?"

"Uh…" Tucker's heart lurched into high gear. He'd been so sure he'd never hear from Lacey again, and he had trouble wrapping his mind around this new development. "Yeah, I did. I hope that's okay."

"It's more than okay. Mom's been chewing my ass about why I didn't invite her when I went over there to get you. I wish I'd known you invited her. I could've saved myself some grief. Oh, and tell her to bring an overnight case. Mom won't hear of you taking her back tonight. Too cold."

"She might not go for that."

"Then you'll have to use your manly charm to convince her. Since the fence is still down, you can take the shortcut. I expect to see you both back here ASAP."

"You want me to go now?" Tucker glanced at the bunkhouse clock. "It's only one. I thought dinner wasn't until four."

"That's the official time the food will be on the table, but... hang on." Jack lowered the phone and called out to someone that he had the situation in hand. Then he was back. "Did you hear that? They're bugging me about this lady. What's her name again?"

"Lacey Evans."

"Yeah, Lacey. Gabe and Nick think they remember her from school. Anyway, you need to produce this woman before I end up in some serious shit for lacking good manners. Take one of the snowmobiles. But don't wreck it, okay?"

"I won't. And I'll pay for fixing—"

"Ah, hell, don't worry about it. I just can't afford to lose another one of those machines in the middle of snow season. See you soon, buddy, with the girl." With that, Jack ended the call.

Tucker hung up the phone, but he was so distracted that he walked out of the bunkhouse minus his hat and coat. The freezing weather sent him right back in to retrieve them. He'd have to snap out of it or he really would wreck another snowmobile.

Forcing himself to concentrate on one thing at a time, he eventually found himself headed across the snowy meadow in the same direction he'd gone the day before when he'd chased Houdini as far as the fence. He and Jack had retraced this route going back to the ranch, so by now the snowmobile had created a recognizable path in the snow.

That was fortunate for Tucker, who thought far more about Lacey than he thought about driving the snowmobile. He'd worked so hard to banish her from his mind earlier today because he'd been convinced she was reuniting with Lenny. Apparently not. And that meant... he didn't know what that meant, or rather, he was afraid to speculate for fear he'd be slammed again.

No smoke came from the chimney as he approached the cabin, which was a good thing. She couldn't go off and leave a fire burning. But then, she'd know that, being a Forest Service employee.

His chest tightened as he parked the snowmobile near the porch. She'd shoveled most of the snow from the steps and he wished he'd been here to help her. He wished he could walk through that door, close it, and stay right here instead of carting her back across the snow to the ranch house where he'd have to share her with a whole lot of people.

As he mounted the steps, the blood rushed in his ears. He hadn't been this nervous about seeing a woman in... he'd never been this nervous, come to think of it.

She opened the door. "Thanks for coming to get me." She stood there looking ready to party in a bright red sweater and crisp jeans. She even had on makeup and gold hoop earrings.

"What happened to Lenny?" He hadn't meant to blurt it out like that, but it was uppermost on his mind and apparently he'd lost control of his tongue. "I thought he was coming out here."

"You thought wrong." She stepped back from the door. "Come in for a minute, Tucker. I have something to say."

He struggled to breathe normally, and when he finally dragged in some air, he got a whiff of the peppermint soap scent clinging to her. He wanted to gobble her up. He took off his hat, mostly so he'd have something to do with his hands.

She closed the door and turned to him. "Tucker, about Lenny. I—"

"Sarah Chance wants you to bring an overnight bag," he said, deliberately interrupting her. He didn't want to hear about Lenny. Maybe Lenny had been delayed and was coming tomorrow, so Lacey had decided to accept the dinner invitation, after all. "Sarah thinks it's too cold for you to come home tonight, so she's inviting you to stay at the ranch house."

"That sounds great. Now, let me tell you about Lenny."

"I don't want to hear about Lenny, okay? If you've decided to go back to him, that's your business. It has nothing to do with me, so—"

"Tucker, shut up." Walking over to him, she grabbed his face in both hands, pulled his head down, and kissed him, hard. The kiss was over in a second and she backed away again. Her eyes glittered as she looked up at him. "Get this straight, cowboy. I don't want Lenny."

"You don't?" An avalanche of relief made him dizzy.

"No. I want you."

He stared at her, not quite willing to trust what he thought he'd just heard.

"I'm taking a chance that you like me enough to give us a shot," she continued. "I realize you're not normally a one-woman man, or at least you didn't used to be when I knew you before, but I'd like you to consider—"

"Yes." He tossed his hat across the room where it landed, he hoped, somewhere in the vicinity of the couch. Then he wrapped both arms around her.

"Yes, what?"

"Yes to being a one-woman man, if you're the woman."

Her beautiful mouth curved in a soft smile. "That's pretty much what I had in mind. I... seem to be falling in love with you."

"Dear God, if this is a dream, I don't want to wake up."

She reached up and pinched his earlobe.

"Ow! What was that for?"

"You're not dreaming."

Still doubting his senses, he gazed down at her. "I must be. The woman I'm falling in love with just said she's falling in love with me."

She went very still. "You're falling in love with me?"

"Yeah." He combed his fingers through her glossy curls. "It's been going on for years, and after the time we've shared in this cabin, it's officially a full-blown case. But I was so sure when Lenny called that you—"

"Why? After our special Christmas, how could you think that I'd go running back to a jerk like Lenny?"

"Because it's happened... a few times before. It seems that I'm generally viewed as a short-term kind of guy."

Her blue gaze grew soft. "Like the girl at the formal, who used you to make her boyfriend jealous?"

"Yeah, or the woman who needed some hot sex to feel better about herself, or the woman who decided that I was fun, but her ex had better career prospects. I could give you more examples, but you get the idea."

"Oh, Tucker." She stroked his cheeks with her thumbs. "No wonder you didn't believe in me. But you will. I promise you will."

He looked into her eyes and saw the love shining there. Only a fool would doubt it. Leaning down, he feathered a gentle kiss over her lips. "I already do believe in you, Lacey." And he kissed her again.

She drew back and placed her finger against his mouth. "Don't we have a party to go to?"

"Good point." Reluctantly he released her, pulled his cell phone out of his coat pocket, and hit the speed dial number for the ranch. He wasn't sure who answered because the noise level was so high. "This is Tucker." He winked at Lacey. "We'll be a little late for the party. Something came up." He disconnected really fast because Lacey had started laughing.

"What?" Dropping the phone back in his coat pocket, he grinned at her as he began unbuttoning his coat.

"You don't think that was too broad a hint?"

"I don't care if it was." He hung his coat on a peg by the door. "It's Christmas and everyone should be allowed to celebrate however they choose." He pulled her close. "Merry Christmas, Lacey."

She smiled up at him. "Merry Christmas, Tucker."

And as he kissed her, he thought about the many Christmas holidays they would celebrate together. They would all be special, because they'd rediscovered the magic of Christmas. But this day, the day they discovered the magic of their love, would always be the most special of all.

IT'S ABOUT TIME, COWBOY

COWBOY

SONS OF CHANCE

Vicki Lewis Thompson

Ocean Dance Press

1

Langford Hutchinson had been known as *Hutch* ever since he'd turned five and demanded a better handle from his parents. They'd named him Langford after a long-dead ancestor who'd been the first Hutchinson to settle in Shoshone, a little town in the Jackson Hole area of Wyoming.

But that bit of history hadn't carried any weight with Ronald and Susan's only son. Even at five he'd known that a name like Langford would get his ass kicked once he started school and he'd wanted to avoid that.

Other than objecting to the unfortunate name choice, Hutch hadn't quibbled much with his parents over the years. But as he stood behind the counter of the Shoshone Feed Store trying to make sense of the day's receipts collected by his father, his frustration escalated into the red zone. No wonder his mother had handled all the transactions.

But she'd been gone for more than a year, a year in which Hutch had put his career as a California-based videographer on hold. He'd come home to help his grief-stricken dad with the store. Truthfully he'd needed some time off to grieve, as well, so it had been a logical move, and his dad loved having him there.

Unfortunately his dad also insisted on being in charge of the cash register, a job for which he had no talent. Consequently Hutch had spent countless afternoons tearing his hair out trying to reconcile the receipts. They had the same goal — for his dad to learn how to run the store properly so Hutch could go back to his career. But his dad wasn't a numbers guy and should probably sell the business.

He didn't want to for many reasons, and Hutch understood that. Losing his wife of forty years was tough enough without losing the store, too. It gave his dad a sense of identity and social contact, both of which he needed right now.

But honest to God, some days Hutch felt like heading back to California and letting his dad sink or swim. He couldn't make himself do it, but something had to change.

For the first few months he'd been helping out, his dad had been there at the end of the day to answer questions about the mess he'd created. Recently, though, his dad had developed the habit of strolling around town an hour or so before closing time, probably to avoid having to explain his screwups to his son.

Yesterday Hutch had bought walkie-talkies and handed one to his father with instructions to carry it during his afternoon ramble. Time to test that program. Picking up his unit, Hutch paged his dad. When a cheerful beep sounded from under a stack of papers beneath the counter, Hutch used up most of the swear words he knew as he crouched down and pulled out the useless walkie-talkie his dad had left there.

"Got a problem?"

He recognized that voice. Glancing up, he met a familiar brown-eyed gaze. He hadn't seen Katrina Bledsoe in years, but she still had the power to set his pulse racing. He'd always had a thing for her, but she was the little sis of Nash Bledsoe, his good buddy, so he'd restrained himself.

He stumbled a little in his haste to stand up. "Hey, there, Trina! I didn't know you were back in town." She'd cut her hair, and he missed the long ripple of it, but the color was still a glossy brown and the short bob looked good on her. He automatically checked her left hand. No ring. Nice to know.

She blessed him with one of her wide, happy smiles. "Just got in today. It was past time for a Mom visit. She comes to New York a fair bit, but I haven't been back here in way too long."

"Still training those thoroughbreds for the racing circuit?"

"Yep. Exciting stuff. Livingston Stables had a horse finish third in the Derby this year."

"That's awesome, Trina."

"Yeah, it was quite a thrill for all of us. We have a tight-knit bunch of trainers. They're covering for me now, but I have to go back at the end of the week. So what's up with you? I just talked to your dad, and he told me that you—"

"You talked to my dad? Where the hell is he?"

She acted surprised that he had to ask. "Over at Lickity Split with my mother."

"Oh." Then he thought about how she'd phrased her answer. It didn't sound as if his dad had simply stopped in for an ice cream cone, although he was fond of them. "What do you mean he's *with* your mother?"

"I mean he's helping her behind the counter, like he's been doing for the past few weeks, according to her. In fact, that's the main reason I'm in Shoshone. I needed to assure Mom face-to-face that she has every right to find happiness with another..." She paused and caught her breath. "Uh-oh. You don't know a thing about this, do you?"

"A thing about what?"

"My mother and your father are sweet on each other."

He stared at her. "No, they're not."

"I beg your pardon, Hutch, but I've just left the ice cream parlor, and the winks and nudges were flying. I think he might have pinched her butt one time, but I can't be absolutely sure about it."

Although he heard every word she'd said, none of it made sense. Surely if his father had a crush on Lucy Bledsoe, owner of the Lickity Split Ice Cream Parlor, he would have noticed.

Trina groaned. "Listen, I'm sorry. You probably aren't ready to hear that. It's only been a year, and I'm sure you can't imagine your dad being interested in anyone other than your mom. I know when my dad passed away I refused to think of Mom finding someone else. But that was seven years ago, and now I—"

"It's not that." Hutch struggled to find his place in this bizarre conversation. "Okay, maybe it's a little bit that. But I live with the guy! Sure, he's on the ground floor of the house and I'm in my old room upstairs, but we spend *lots* of time together. I can't believe that he has some hot romance going that I don't know about."

"I'm not saying it's consummated or anything." Then she glanced at him in horror. "Forget I said that."

"Already forgotten. Erased, just like with *Men in Black*."

"I mean, it's not something you want to think about your parents doing."

"No kidding. Let's drop the subject, okay?"

"Fine with me." She surveyed the receipts on the counter. "How close are you to finishing up? I'd love to buy you a drink at the Spirits and Spurs."

"I'll take care of this later." Scooping everything into a pile, he found a manila envelope under the counter and shoved the receipts inside. Then he grabbed the front door key and came out from behind the counter. "Let's go."

"Excellent! I admire a decisive man."

Hutch laughed as he walked with her to the door. "I don't know about you, but I could use a drink."

"Judging from your vocabulary choices when I first came in and the bombshell I just dropped on you, I'll bet you could. Are you finding time to film your videos? Nash has kept me semi-updated on your wild and crazy life, so I didn't expect to see you behind the counter of the feed store tallying receipts."

"It's a long story." He opened the door for her. "And as for that drink, I'm buying."

"But I invited you."

Flipping the sign on the door from Open to Closed, he locked up and pocketed the key. "You've been back East too long, little lady. You're in the West, now, and in these parts, the men do the buying."

"That's ridiculous, but if it makes you feel like a macho cowboy, go for it."

"It does." He'd always loved her sassy attitude. And her cute little ass. And her full mouth, which he'd never tasted. He'd thought about it, even dreamed about it, but he hadn't been ready to settle down and Nash would have demanded a wedding if Hutch had slept with his sister.

In Shoshone, Wyoming, a guy didn't seduce his best friend's sister and then leave her high and dry. Not if he wanted to keep his teeth. So he'd never acted on his attraction to Trina Bledsoe, but times had changed. She'd invited him for a drink. And Nash wasn't here.

* * *

Trina felt like an insensitive jerk for blurting out the news about her mother and Hutch's dad, so she was relieved that Hutch was up for a drink at the Spirits and Spurs, Shoshone's only tavern and a favorite watering hole for the residents. Which of them bought the drinks wasn't important, but a nice long chat would give her a chance to smooth over her faux pas.

Hutch was the last person on earth she wanted to make feel uncomfortable. She'd had a soft spot for him — or more accurately a *hot* spot for him — since she'd turned thirteen and realized that boys weren't so bad, after all. Suddenly her big brother's friends, two years older than she was, had become fascinating to her, especially Hutch, whose dark hair and green eyes had starred in most of her teenage fantasies. She'd never had the nerve to confess that to anyone, although Nash had figured it out.

Hutch's dedication and enterprising spirit had impressed her almost as much as how fine he looked in a pair of jeans. When a film crew had arrived in Jackson Hole to shoot footage of extreme winter sports during Hutch's senior year, he'd spent every free moment trailing after them.

He'd mastered the basics by the time they'd left, and that summer he'd produced a video of himself hang-gliding, a camera strapped to his chest. As he'd continued his daredevil stunts to get amazing videos, he'd won the hearts of all the girls in town, including Trina's.

Nash had warned her off, saying Hutch wouldn't be tying himself down to any woman for a long, long time. Trina had wanted to argue that she wasn't looking for long-term. A temporary thrill would have suited her just fine. But she couldn't say such a thing to her brother, who'd always been overprotective. And she hadn't wanted to cause problems between Nash and his good friend Hutch.

"I don't know how I missed hearing that you were back home working with your dad," she said as they walked the short distance to the Spirits and Spurs. She tried not to ogle him, but he looked so darned good. His faded jeans, leather cowboy boots and yoked Western shirt were common around here, but Hutch wore the clothes better than most.

"I'm going to blame my lack of info on Nash," she continued. "He knows, right?"

"He does, but he probably didn't mention it because this was supposed to be temporary. I only meant to stay a couple of months until Dad got used to running the store by himself."

"I can't believe you've been enjoying the experience." She increased her pace to keep up with his long-legged stride. "The Hutch I knew would have been bored out of his skull clerking at a feed store."

"Which I am." He pushed open the door to the Spirits and Spurs and ushered her inside.

"But you're still here," she said over her shoulder.

"Turns out Dad's great at schmoozing with the customers, but the financial aspects of the business elude him. Mom used to handle that. I didn't realize that she did it out of necessity until she was gone and the whole operation fell to pieces." He paused. "Booth, table, or bar stool?"

Trina took in the cozy ambience of a place that was one of two social centers in town, the Shoshone Diner being the other. A handful of people had already gathered for happy hour — two cowboys at the curved wooden bar, three women at a table and a young couple in one of the booths lining the room.

Trina recognized the couple as Lickity Split customers, but she didn't know any of the others. Years ago she could have identified everyone in town and most of the dogs and horses, too. Not anymore.

"Booth." She walked toward one in the far corner.

"Works for me."

A young waitress who obviously had a crush on Hutch came over to take their order. Trina empathized with the girl's calf-eyed adoration and hoped she'd been more subtle at that age. Probably not, though. Hutch seemed oblivious.

After the waitress left with an order for two drafts and a bowl of peanuts, a woman with a long blond braid came out of an office on the far side of the room. Now here was someone Trina knew well. Josie owned the Spirits and Spurs.

She'd also married the oldest Chance boy, Jack, the summer before last. Trina hadn't been able to make it back for the wedding, but Nash had driven over from Sacramento. Nash, Hutch and Jack had been close friends through high school and into their twenties. Jack was the first to get married, and now he and Josie had a baby boy.

Josie's casual glance around the room grew more focused when she spotted Trina and Hutch. With a smile, she walked over to their booth. "Trina!"

Trina stood to give her a hug. "How are you, Josie?"

"Terrific. Tired but happy." She glanced over at Hutch, who had risen to his feet at Josie's approach. "Sit, sit, both of you. I can't stay long, anyway. Lucy told me you were coming for a visit, Trina. When can you head out to the Last Chance for a ride?"

"You name a time and I'll be there. Riding at the Last Chance is such a treat for me."

"In the morning, around nine?"

"Sounds great. And you look wonderful, Josie." Trina beamed at her. "Motherhood obviously agrees with you. How's Jack coping with being a daddy?"

Josie's expression softened. "It's beautiful to watch. I wondered if he'd guard his emotions because of his own trauma as a kid, but little Archie is his whole world."

Hutch nodded. "He's plain nuts about that baby. And speaking of Jack's tough childhood, has anyone heard from that guy from San Francisco who showed up last year claiming to be his half-brother?"

"A half-brother?" Trina's eyes widened. "Boy, I'm really out of the loop."

"Not a lot of people know about it," Josie said.

"Does my mom?" Trina needed to have a talk with both her mom and her brother about relaying important news from Shoshone.

"Maybe not," Josie said. "It's no big secret, and it might amount to nothing. Last summer Wyatt Locke appeared at the ranch and announced that Diana, who abandoned Jack when he was two and seemed to disappear from the face of the earth, moved to San Francisco, remarried and gave birth to twin boys, Wyatt and Rafe."

"And Jack was blindsided by the news," Hutch said quietly. "We had a beer one night and he told me Wyatt said he might be back this summer and he might not. Jack wasn't sure which he wanted to happen. That's why I wondered if he'd made contact."

"Not so far." Josie sighed. "But now that Wyatt's opened this can of worms, he shouldn't leave Jack hanging. It needs to be resolved." She turned as the waitress arrived with two foaming mugs. "Your beer's arrived, and I have to scoot. See you in the morning. You, too, Hutch, if you can make it. How long are you staying, Trina?"

"Four days."

"That's barely enough time to say hi and goodbye."

"I know. But it's all I can spare."

"I'm sure you're in demand at the track. Whoops, there's my cell. Later!" Pulling a phone out of her jeans pocket, she put it to her ear as she walked away.

Hutch leaned across the table. "Only four days?"

"Yep."

The glow of interest in his eyes grew brighter. "Then I guess you'll have to make the most of it."

Her thoughts, exactly. Without Nash here, they could finally scratch that itch.

2

From the moment Hutch had looked up to find Trina leaning over the feed store's counter, he'd been thinking about using this golden opportunity to spend time alone with her without worrying about Nash's disapproval. He hadn't realized he'd be on such a tight timeline, though.

Picking up his frosty mug, he lifted it in her direction. "To renewing old friendships."

"I'll drink to that." Trina clinked mugs with him and took a sip that left a mustache of foam on her upper lip. She licked it off with a grin. "I'm out of practice drinking from a mug. Usually I'm sipping it from a bottle while I'm sitting around the barn with the other trainers."

"And you're in your element there, I'll bet."

"I'd say so, yes."

"That's something I always admired about you, Trina. You're down-to-earth."

She blinked. "You admired me? Since when?"

"Since..." He stopped to think. "I guess the first time I noticed you was the summer between my junior and senior year."

She pointed a finger at him. "And I'll bet I can guess when. It was the day my mother made you, Nash and Jack take me along to the swimming hole. I'd been driving her crazy and she wanted me out of her hair."

"That's the day, all right. You wore a bright yellow bikini." He could still picture her in it. The memory had an effect on him even now, and his groin tightened.

"My mother had no idea that's what I had on under my jeans and tank top. She thought I'd worn the virginal white one-piece she'd bought me in Jackson. When Nash saw that bikini, he was not happy."

"I was."

"Really? Then why did you treat me like a bratty little tagalong all day?"

He took a fortifying sip of his beer and set it back on the scarred wooden table. "Because you were Nash's little sister, and if he'd guessed what I was thinking, he would have cleaned my clock."

She gazed at him in obvious fascination. "You wanted me back then?"

"With the heat of a thousand suns."

"Damn it, Hutch! If I'd known that, it would have changed my entire image of myself. My high school career would have been completely different. It would have—"

"Landed us both in a heap of trouble. You were *fifteen*. You weren't ready for the kind of action I had in mind." He should probably stop talking about this. The more he did, the more this little booth warmed up, and he didn't have a plan.

"Meanwhile you were a worldly *seventeen*." She took another drink of her beer. "I'll bet you were still a virgin."

"No, I wasn't." He hadn't meant to say that, but there was no taking it back, now.

"Is that so?" Her eyebrows lifted. "Do I know her?"

"A gentleman doesn't discuss such things."

"Oh, come on, Hutch. I'll tell you who my first was if you'll tell me yours. On second thought, let me guess. Candice Melbourne."

He did his best to stare her down without giving anything away, but apparently he failed.

"It *was* her. I can tell by the way your eye is twitching. She had the biggest rack in the junior class. Of course you'd go for her."

"I refuse to confirm or deny."

Trina began to laugh. "Okay, then, I'm not telling you who was my first."

He suddenly had a burning desire to know. Then again, knowing might be a bad thing. If the guy was still in town, Hutch would rather *not* know. What if he was someone Hutch actually liked? That would end any potential friendship, because he couldn't imagine being friends with anyone who had—

"Simon Flear."

Hutch groaned. "Not *him*."

"Why not? He had a poet's soul. He used to write odes to my beauty. You Neanderthals didn't appreciate someone who was a million times more sensitive to a woman's needs than you were."

Hutch shook his head in disbelief. "The guy had no *cojones*."

"Oh, yes, he did. In fact, he had very impressive—"

"Don't tell me. I don't want to hear about it." He gulped more beer. "When did this take place?"

"I thought you didn't want to hear about it."

"I just need some historic perspective."

"He took me to my senior prom. He came home from college specifically so he could do that. I was touched."

Hutch grimaced. "In the head. You know, I would have gladly taken you to your senior prom." And now he wished he had, if only to save her from Simon.

"But you didn't ask, did you?"

"No, because Nash would have demanded to know my intentions, and if I'd told him the truth, he would have knocked me clear into next week. He never suspected that Simon was a threat to your innocence."

"I can testify that Simon is absolutely heterosexual."

"Yay." He polished off his beer.

As if the waitress had been watching his every move, she appeared by his elbow. "Another round?"

"Fine with me. Trina?"

"Sounds good," Trina said. "But I need to call my mother and tell her I won't be home for dinner." She pulled out her phone, but then she paused and glanced questioningly at Hutch. "I'm assuming we'll move on to dinner?"

"Absolutely. I have to make up for lost time and Simon Flear."

Trina laughed, which made her brown eyes go all sparkly. "That was a long time ago."

"Yeah, but when I look at you, it seems like yesterday." Nothing had changed, either. He still wanted her with the heat of a thousand suns.

Her gaze met his. "I know what you mean. The roads not taken and all that."

"And now you're building a life hundreds of miles away." He had to ask the next question and make sure he wasn't misreading the light in her eyes. "Anyone special back there?"

"No." Her sweet mouth curved. "But there's someone special right here."

His heart slammed against his ribs. She was picking up his cues. "You'd better call your mother. Tell her..."

"Not to wait up?"

Whew. He hadn't had an adrenaline rush like this since he'd run the rapids on the Snake River. "Right. Tell her that."

* * *

Trina hoped she looked calmer than she felt. Her finger shook and she almost dialed the wrong number on her phone. Unless she didn't know men at all, Hutch was planning a seduction. And she was more than willing to be seduced after years of imagining Hutch making love to her.

Her mother's phone went to voicemail, so she left a vague message about meeting up with an old friend and needing time to catch up. Well, that was partly true.

She disconnected and tucked the phone back in her pocket. "Maybe you should call your dad and let him know you're set for dinner."

"Can't. He refuses to carry a phone. That's why I decided to try a walkie-talkie, because it's not as complicated, but he didn't take that with him today, either. That's what I was cussing about when you walked in. I honestly don't know what I'm going to do with him."

Trina had some ideas, but she wasn't sure Hutch was ready to hear them because they involved her mother. "Something has to happen. You're wasting your talents clerking in a feed store."

"I don't know about that, but I sure do miss the excitement of making those videos. You may not have time to go online, but—"

"Are you kidding? I probably own every video you've made. In fact, I was wondering when I'd get a notice of new ones coming out. Now I understand why there's a holdup."

"My PR guy isn't too happy about it, either. I've explained that I can't leave until I'm sure my dad can make it without me."

"You really can't." She wondered if Hutch would be able to accept a solution that involved having another woman step into his mother's shoes. But mentioning that now would be premature. She glanced up and smiled at the waitress who'd arrived with two more drafts. "We'll need menus."

"Coming right up." The girl's attention swung immediately to Hutch. "Although you usually order a hamburger medium well with all the fixings. I can get that started for you."

"That'll be fine, but Trina will want to look at the menu."

"Not really." Trina fought not to laugh. Hutch had no idea that the waitress was about to fall at his feet. "Make it two hamburgers."

After the waitress left, Trina lowered her voice. "She has a huge crush on you."

He looked startled. "Me? I'm almost old enough to be—"

"Her older brother. Age doesn't matter to her, though. If anything, it makes you more glamorous. She has it bad." She gave him a rueful smile. "Reminds me of myself at her age."

"I don't see that at all. You were never boy crazy."

"That's how much you know. I was crazy as a bedbug. Over you."

He looked genuinely surprised. "You *were*? But you never said anything."

"That's right, I didn't."

He picked up his beer mug. "Probably better that way. Any encouragement from you, and I would have said to hell with Nash's disapproval."

"Which is exactly why I didn't let on. I knew it would cause problems between you two."

He gazed at her over the rim of his mug. "I can't believe you felt like that back then. I honestly had no idea."

"I did my best to hide it. Besides, as we've just established, you don't pick up on those things very well."

"Apparently not." He sipped his beer. "But if I had, it would have changed everything."

"And our timing would have been all wrong."

Setting down his beer, he reached for her hand, cradling it in both of his and stroking her palm with his thumb. "So tell me, Trina, how's our timing now?"

Her hand tingled in the warmth of his grip. His hands were large and roughened from handling fifty-pound sacks of grain and slinging bales of hay. She quivered at the thought of feeling those hands on her naked body.

Seeing the hot flare of lust in his green eyes, she grew moist and achy. This encounter was long overdue, and they owed it to themselves to enjoy the moment. "You know, Hutch, I think our timing's just about perfect."

<u>3</u>

Hutch lost all interest in food at that point. But they'd ordered the hamburgers and if they left without eating them, people would talk. They might, anyway, because not many secrets survived in this little town.

Frankly he didn't give a damn if people knew, but Trina might. From the corner of his eye he saw the waitress arriving with two plates of food. Giving Trina's hand a squeeze, he released it and sat back in the booth.

The waitress's movements were brisk and her manner wasn't nearly as friendly as it had been. Now that he understood the situation, he could imagine why. She'd seen him holding Trina's hand and didn't much like that.

After she stomped away, Trina ducked her head to hide a grin.

"Yeah, I know. She's jealous." Hutch waited for Trina to use the ketchup and mustard before doctoring his own burger. "I swear to you, I've never given that girl any reason to think I'm interested."

"She doesn't need that to create her rich fantasy life. Trust me, I know all about it." She took a bite of her hamburger.

"I'm still getting used to this concept. You actually had a fantasy life involving me?"

Still chewing, she nodded.

"I don't know if I can handle that kind of pressure."

She swallowed and dabbed at her mouth with a napkin. "You think you have pressure? I'm about to have an encounter with a man who became a legend in his own time, a man who started out with the likes of Candice Melbourne. I've never had a body like that, not even when I was seventeen."

If she only knew how often he'd fantasized about her body in that yellow bikini. "Figures like Candice's are overrated. At seventeen, that's what I thought I wanted. But Trina, you've always had the best ass in Wyoming. I thought so back then and I still do."

"Now you're making me blush."

"Good. You look great with color in your cheeks. Now eat up. I don't want to spend the whole night sitting in this booth."

"Which brings up another issue."

"You're saying this could get a little tricky?" He took another generous bite of his burger.

"Neither of us has our own place. I'm sleeping on the pull-out sofa at Mom's."

He finished chewing and swallowed. "At least I have a room with a door on it. Or maybe we should take a drive to Jackson." He quickly rejected that idea. "Nope. Drive's too long. Getting through this meal is bad enough without adding another hour on the road."

"We could act like teenagers and park somewhere."

"Dealing with this problem makes me feel like a teenager, but I'll be damned if we're going to do it in a car or the back of a pickup. Keep eating. I'll think of something." The more he wrestled with the problem, the more he knew that his bedroom was their best bet.

It was the nearest spot with a good innerspring, and he had a box of condoms up there. With luck his dad would be watching TV with the volume blasting, and if they came in through the back, his dad would never notice Trina quietly going upstairs while Hutch distracted him. There were advantages to having parents whose ears weren't as sharp as they once were.

Pushing back his plate, he reached for the wallet in his back pocket. He knew the prices by heart and didn't need a bill to figure what he owed. "If you're ready to leave, I have a plan." And thinking about it had added considerably to his lust level.

As she stood, she gave him a teasing glance. "Sure you don't want to stay for dessert?"

"The dessert I have in mind isn't on the menu." He took her hand, not caring if anyone noticed, and hurried her out the door.

* * *

"Where are we going, exactly?" Trina was out of breath, both from the fast pace Hutch had set and the prospect of what would happen once they reached their destination. Because he was leading her through alleys and down unpaved side streets, she'd lost all sense of direction.

"To my dad's house using shortcuts."

"Won't he still be up?"

"Sure, but we can get around that if we go in through the kitchen. By now, Dad's eating dinner in front of the TV in the living room. I'll go make polite conversation while you walk quietly upstairs. My bedroom's the first door on the right."

"Now I *really* feel like a teenager trying to put one over on the parents."

He glanced down at her. "Is that a bad thing?"

"Actually, no. It's the best of both worlds — teenage excitement without the teenage angst." She'd never approached the Hutchinson house from the back, only stared dreamily at it from the street side, longing for her idol to appear.

But once the house came in view, she recognized the neat white two-story that looked as if the siding and dark green shutters had recently been repainted. "Are you keeping up the house, or your dad?"

"I am. And that's fine. I could easily come home for a week in the summer and spruce up the place. The store is the big problem, and I don't have the heart to talk him into selling. I don't know what he'd do with himself without that store."

Trina suspected Ronald would get along just fine with the feed store if he had a businesswoman like her mother helping out, but once again, she didn't say so. She needed to have another talk with her mom before she made any such statements to Hutch.

When they reached the steps going up to the small porch outside the kitchen door, Hutch stopped. "Wait here while I scope things out. I suppose he could still be microwaving his dinner."

"Does he eat microwave dinners every night?"

"Pretty much. My cooking skills are limited and he never learned. I'll be right back."

As Hutch went through the kitchen door, Trina thought about her mother's love of cooking, a passion that had no satisfactory outlet because she lived alone. Cooking meals for a man who existed on microwave dinners would hold a powerful appeal for her. No wonder romance was in the air.

Hutch opened the kitchen door and beckoned to her. "I don't know where he is, but he's not in the house. Guess we lucked out."

Trina smiled but kept her suspicions to herself. "Guess so."

"I see that look. You think he's with your mother, don't you?"

"I do." She walked up the steps. "When I left her a message that I wouldn't be home for dinner, she probably fixed him a meal, or else they went out to the diner. I think it's sweet."

"I think it's convenient." He pulled her through the door and into his arms. "Come here, you."

Her pulse leaped as her body made contact with his solid warmth. Ah, he felt good. "Shouldn't we get upstairs while the getting's good?"

"If you're right about where my dad's hanging out, and you probably are, then I have time to kiss you first." He pulled her in tight, allowing her to feel his erection. "And I've waited years for the chance."

"Years?" Heart pounding, she wound both arms around his neck and breathed in the remembered aroma of his shaving lotion. Now it was mixed with the scent of arousal, both his and hers. Her voice quivered slightly. "Come to think of it, I've waited years, too."

Combing her hair back and cupping her cheek in one hand, he tilted her mouth up to meet his. "Then I'd better make this good." He leaned down, but then he drew back to gaze at her. "You're not closing your eyes."

"After all the anticipation, I don't want to miss anything."

His mouth tilted at the corners. "There's more to a kiss than what you see."

"I know, but—"

"Trina, don't mess me up here. Close your eyes." He kissed her forehead, and as his warm breath tickled her lashes, she lowered them.

"Thank you. Don't want you staring up my nostrils."

She started to giggle.

"Oh, hell, don't do that. This is supposed to be serious stuff." He pressed his mouth gently against each eyelid.

She swallowed a bubble of laughter. "Okay."

"Don't get me wrong." He kissed his way down to her cheek. "I love your laugh. It's one of the sweetest sounds in the world to me."

Wow.

"I just don't want you to laugh right now." He kissed her other cheek and moved to her jaw.

Any thoughts of doing that drifted away the longer he held her close. She stood very still and absorbed the amazing sensation of his lips feathering her skin. Hutch's lips. The moment had a dreamlike quality, especially because he moved with such careful reverence, as if he, too, cherished every second and didn't want to miss a single square inch of her face before he finally touched her mouth.

If this turned out to be a dream, she was going to be pissed.

Then he made contact with her mouth, and she knew it was real, so real that she gasped at the raw power of it. With a moan, he thrust with his tongue, and she was lost, carried away on a tide of passion so strong that she lost track of where she was.

Nothing mattered but his hot, demanding mouth. He held her with a surety and strength that allowed her to let go of all control. When he swept her up in his arms, she accepted that as inevitable, even though no man had ever carried her up a flight of stairs in her life. But this was Hutch, and with him, anything was possible.

As instructed, she kept her eyes closed. She heard him kick his bedroom door closed and felt the mattress under her back as he laid her on it. He put his mouth against her ear. "Let me lock the door, for good measure."

Then he was gone, and she opened her eyes at last. Outside his curtained bedroom window, twilight had descended and transformed her surroundings from color to shades of gray. But she could still make out the trappings of a room that had once belonged to a teenager. Sports pennants and posters lined the walls, and the furniture was sturdy and plain.

He walked back to the double bed, unsnapping his shirt as he approached. "You look so right in my bed."

"Your dad could come home any minute, right?"

"Yep." He pulled off his boots and tossed them aside. "So we're going to be very..." Leaning down, he nibbled on her mouth. "Very, very, very... quiet."

Reaching up, she buried her fingers in his luxurious dark hair and pulled him closer for a more soul-satisfying kiss.

"Mmm." He slid one hand under the hem of her knit top and cupped her cotton-covered breast while he explored the center section with his thumb as if looking for a clasp.

Wishing she'd worn something sexier today, she broke their kiss for a moment. "Back fastener," she murmured.

"I like it." His breath was warm against her face as he slipped his hand behind her back and undid the hooks and eyes. "My no-frills Trina."

"I can have frills."

"But you don't need them." With a sigh, he cradled her breast and slowly stroked his thumb over her nipple. "You're perfect just the way you are."

She would have liked to make some intelligent response to that, but her brain had just turned to mush. Hutch was fondling her breast, and she was so transfixed by that realization that she couldn't speak. He was good at this. He was very, very... Then he pushed her top and bra up so he could... oh, my. That was one wicked mouth he had.

Arching upward, she silently offered him more, anything he wanted, in fact. He could put that talented mouth anywhere he had a mind to.

And so he did. Her clothes melted away as if by magic, and he proceeded to turn her inside out with his mouth, his tongue and a dexterity that made him a good videographer and an even better lover.

When his explorations took him to that special place between her thighs, and she realized that having his mouth and tongue right there would have a predictable result, she gasped out a request. "Pillow."

"For your head?"

"For my screams."

"Ah." He reached for one and handed it to her. "Here."

"Thanks. Proceed."

"As if you could stop me now."

As if she'd want to. His goal was hers, and when he achieved it, she yelled into the pillow while rainbows and confetti rained down. And she wondered, when life returned to normal as it always did, how she'd ever live without the pleasure of making love with Hutch.

Trailing kisses back up her quaking body, he eased the pillow away. "Wish I could have heard that."

She drew in a shaky breath. "I would have broken your eardrums."

"We're not done, you know." His voice was thick with need.

"I hope not." She gulped for air. "But in all the excitement, I didn't stop to think that you might not have—"

"I do." He held up a small foil packet that she could see, even in the fading light.

"Were you expecting someone?"

"No. I just..." He lifted a shoulder in an easy shrug. "What can I say? I was a Boy Scout."

"Thank goodness for that." Trina felt the sap rising in her eager veins once again. "If you'll suit up, I'm all for another round."

"So soon?"

"Hutch, I have a ton of fantasies stored away. We've only scratched the surface."

4

Hutch wasn't sure what he'd done to deserve the gift of Trina lying in his bed while the house happened to be empty and he was in possession of several condoms. But he wasn't about to let this opportunity go to waste. She had her dream job at a racing stable in New York and he would eventually return to his neglected career, but fate had thrown them together for a few short days.

That was more than he'd ever hoped for with Trina Bledsoe. He wouldn't be greedy and expect some long-term arrangement, but by God, while he had her here, he planned to be as greedy as hell. Rolling on a condom, he climbed back into bed and dropped a kiss on her moist lips.

He'd been in such a hurry to touch her and get her naked that they were still lying on top of his comforter. "I should rearrange things so we're under the covers instead of on top of them," he murmured.

She cupped his face in both hands. "You should rearrange things so you're on top of *me*, locked between my thighs, with your nice big—"

"Okay, okay." He moved into position. "How did you know it was big?"

"Duh. I watched you put on the condom."

"Bigger than Simon Flear's?"

"I only said his family jewels were big. The rest was sort of average."

"Glad to hear it." And with that, he slid into paradise. Apparently he groaned upon entry.

She clapped a hand over his mouth. "Shh!"

He nodded his understanding, and she took her hand away.

"You have to be careful." She sounded endearingly earnest. "I can use a pillow, but that won't work for you."

With the most sensitive part of his anatomy buried in warm, vibrating, sensual comfort, he had trouble being worried about anything. "I could bite on a bullet."

"We don't have one. Plus that never seemed like a good idea. You could choke. But seriously, you have to control yourself."

"Not easy." He rocked his hips and withdrew just enough to feel the friction. This was going to be outstanding. Bellow-worthy. And he couldn't make a sound, damn it.

He checked on Trina, and she was breathing fast. "Good?"

"Yes. But I'm worried. We could get carried away."

"I hope we do." He stroked again and she gasped. Now that was a gratifying reaction. Pausing, he listened carefully. "Hey, there's no TV noise downstairs. If Dad was home, the TV would be on. Let's go for it."

"But—"

"It'll be okay." Without waiting to hear her objections, he began thrusting, deep, steady and with purpose.

She caught fire, rising to meet him. Clutching his back, she wrapped her legs around his hips, giving him access to go deeper. And she began to whimper.

What a glorious sound. He moved faster, ramping up the intensity. The bed creaked, and as he pumped harder, the headboard thumped against the wall with a wild, primitive beat. Her whimpers escalated to moans, and finally became jubilant cries of pleasure.

Yes! This was what he'd wanted! He struggled for breath as he continued to drive into her. They were both slick with sweat, their bodies sliding against each other in a perfect, balanced rhythm. "Come for me, Trina." His voice was hoarse, foreign to his ears. "Come for me!"

She tightened around him and erupted with a loud wail. The headboard crashed against the wall twice more, and he followed her, surging forward to his climax with a shout of triumph.

And then, all was quiet except for their ragged breathing. Hutch leaned his forehead against hers. "I think... we got away with that."

"Yeah." She quivered in his arms. "And even... even if we didn't... it was..."

"Worth it."

"Uh-huh."

Hutch kissed her slowly, with much gratitude. He'd experienced many moments of pure joy in his life. But this... this rivaled them all.

* * *

As dawn brightened the sky outside Hutch's bedroom window, Trina roused herself from a brief nap and turned her head to gaze at her sleeping hero. She was no innocent virgin. She'd had lovers and two serious relationships. But she'd never spent such a passion-filled night with any man.

After their one noisy session, they'd turned down the volume but never the heat. They'd tried unusual positions that left them both helpless with muffled laughter. Then they'd gone back to the soul-shattering communication that went way beyond the term *having sex.* In every sense of the words, they'd made love. All night long.

And now, before the sun came up, she needed to get the heck out of this house. If Hutch's dad was like most men of his generation, he rose early. She needed to beat him to the kitchen, where she'd escape quietly out the back door.

No point in waking Hutch. She'd text him later and they could figure out when and where they'd meet again. Now that she'd experienced lovemaking Hutch-style, she hoped her remaining three days would be filled to the brim with more encounters.

These days were a gift, and she had no illusions that more would come of it. She wasn't about to leave her thoroughbred racing stable to trail around after him, and he made action-packed videos, or would again soon, that tended to be shot out West. They had no room in their lives for each other.

She managed to dress and leave the room quietly carrying her shoes. With one last fond glance at her Adonis lying sprawled face-down on the bed in all his naked glory, she crept toward the stairs. Her mental image of Hutch as she'd left him put a smile on her face. He might think she had the best ass in Wyoming, but she considered him a strong contender for the title.

Halfway to the bottom a stair creaked. She paused to hold her breath and listen for sounds of activity anywhere in the house, but especially in the kitchen. Silence reigned, and she continued on. If she met Hutch's dad before she made her escape, she'd brave it out, but she'd rather not have to.

On the last stair, she heard a door open down the hall. Damn it! As footsteps approached, she briefly considered bolting for the kitchen door, but that could get ugly if the door was locked and she had to fumble with the knob. Being caught fleeing the scene was worse than facing the inevitable with dignity.

She wasn't ashamed of spending the night with Hutch. They were both adults, and they'd acted responsibly and with courtesy for the other inhabitant of the house. Well, except that one time, but surely Ronald hadn't been home to hear that or he would have come up to investigate.

Taking a deep breath, she descended the last step and turned to face the shadowed hallway. "I don't want to scare you, Mr. Hutchinson," she said distinctly.

The footsteps paused.

"It's only me, Katrina Bledsoe. I... spent the night upstairs with your son." Gulp. That had been tougher to say than she'd expected. Not the sort of proclamation she'd ever had to give.

The footsteps continued. "And I spent the night downstairs with his father."

"*Mom?*" Trina stared in disbelief as her mother appeared wearing a plaid flannel bathrobe that didn't belong to her. Her red hair stuck out in all directions, and she had... oh, good Lord, a *hickey*.

"Hello, Katrina." Her mother's gaze was maddeningly calm. "So Hutch was the *old friend*, was he?"

"Never mind that. What the hell are *you* doing here?" Stupid question. She knew the answer, but she didn't want to know she knew.

Her mom's expression changed from benign to stern mother-mode. "You watch your language, young lady!"

"Lucy?" Ronald Hutchinson, a tall, gaunt man with white hair and a neat white mustache, ambled down the hall wearing dog-themed pajamas. "What's all the yelling about? What's Katrina doing here so early?"

Her mother folded her arms. "Ironically, I think she's passing judgment on me."

Ronald put an arm around her mother. "She wouldn't do that, would you, Trina?"

"No! But I hardly expected to find my mother coming down the hall wearing a strange man's bathrobe!"

"He's not a strange man." Her mother gazed fondly up at Ronald. "He's a dear. And also very virile. He—"

"Stop." Trina clapped her hands over her ears. "I don't want any details."

"Any details of what?" Hutch appeared at the top of the stairs wearing only his jeans.

He looked extremely yummy, but also very much like a man who had spent the night in wild abandon. As he padded down the stairs in his bare feet, Trina noticed that he, too, had a hickey.

Her mother glanced from Hutch to Trina. "Well, isn't this cozy?"

Trina waved her hands in the air. "No, it's not cozy. It's totally weird."

Apparently Ronald had just figured out the situation, because he drilled his son with a piercing glance. "Langford, what's been going on under my roof?"

Hutch looked sheepish. "Well, the thing is, Trina and I—"

"I *thought* I heard noises upstairs," her mother said. "I thought it was mice."

"Oh, God." Trina covered her face with both hands. The thought of Hutch's dad hearing something was one thing, but the idea that instead her *mother*... but then again, her mother had also been... no, not going there.

"Son, I need to know what your intentions are toward my future stepdaughter."

Trina dropped her hands to stare at Ronald. "What did you say?"

"It's obvious that my son has put you in a compromising position, Trina, and I want to know what he intends to do about it."

Ronald's protective stance was cute and outdated, but that wasn't the part of his statement she needed explained. "Future *stepdaughter*? Are you saying that you and my mom are getting married?"

"Ronald, you old dog!" Her mom turned to him. "That's the most original proposal I've ever heard. I accept!"

"Hold on a minute." Hutch descended the stairs, his expression thunderous. "Dad, are you seriously telling me that you're at the proposal stage with a woman and you've never said one damned word about it to your only son?"

Ronald had the good grace to look chagrined. "I wasn't sure how you'd take it. You were very close to your mother, and—"

"I thought I was very close to you!"

"Tell you what," her mom said. "We all need coffee. I'll put on the pot, and fry up some bacon and eggs."

"Great idea, Lucy, my dear." Ronald beamed at her. "I could go for some of your specialty eggs. I love the spices you add in."

Trina's gaze swung to Hutch's. If Ronald was used to eating Lucy's specialty eggs in the morning, this wasn't the first time they'd danced the bedroom tango together. Hutch's frown indicated he'd come to the same conclusion.

"Nothing for me, thanks," Trina said. "I need to get going."

"Surely not," her mother said. "You're on vacation. Let's all have breakfast together and talk this out."

"Actually I promised Josie I'd be out at the Last Chance bright and early for a ride. I'm already running late."

"I'll drive you," Hutch said. "Let's meet at your mom's house in twenty minutes." He turned and took the stairs two at a time.

"That's okay," she called after him. "I can drive myself."

He paused on the upstairs landing. "I'll drive you. We need to talk."

Ominous-sounding words, but she knew they did have to talk. Their parents were old-fashioned enough to think that two people who had sex should also have an exclusive, committed relationship. She and Hutch weren't planning on that. So unless they chose to willfully disregard their parents' feelings, which certainly wasn't an option for her, their fling was over.

"Okay, Hutch," she said. "I'll be ready. See you later, Mom. Ronald." With that she hurried through the kitchen and out the back door. She couldn't escape fast enough.

5

Despite the necessity for a serious discussion, Hutch made small talk all the way out to the ranch. He knew what had to be said eventually, knew their brief affair was over, but he didn't want to end it when he couldn't at least give her his full attention. So they delved into the Chance family's doings and all the changes that had taken place for Jack and his two brothers ever since their dad had been killed in a truck rollover several years ago.

"And now Jack might have another change if his half-brother comes back," Hutch said as he drove down to the large, hip-roofed barn not far from the main house.

"You'll have to keep me posted on that. Oh, wait, maybe you'll be heading out soon, yourself..." She trailed off, as if realizing she'd inched close to a conversation they might not be ready to have.

"We'll see." Hutch had called ahead to alert Josie that he was with Trina and they were early. Way early. He said they needed a good hard ride. Two handsome Paints, one brown and white and one black and white, stood saddled and tied to the hitching post.

Jack, dressed in his signature black shirt and jeans, came from the barn. "Got your instructions," he said as he walked toward them. "Josie sends her apologies. She'd hoped to ride with you today, but Archie's got the sniffles."

Hutch accepted Jack's warm handshake. "Hope it's nothing serious."

"Nah. No fever. But she didn't feel right leaving him with someone when he's cranky. So, Trina, how've you been, girl?" Jack gave her an affectionate hug that nearly knocked off her straw cowboy hat. "From the look of you, you're enjoying life on the fast track."

"I am. Listen, thanks for letting us borrow a couple of horses."

"Don't mention it. Patches and Ink Spot will give you a good ride." He untied the brown and white Paint. "I figured Patches for you because she matches your hair and I know color coordination can be so important to a woman."

Trina laughed as she accepted the reins and mounted up. "Absolutely. Can't imagine getting on a horse that clashes with my hair. It's just not cool."

Hutch untied Ink Spot's reins and swung into the saddle. "Thanks again, Jack."

"No problem. And don't hurry back. It's a beautiful morning for a ride. I'd go with you if I didn't have sixty-eleven things to do. See you later." With a wave, he returned to the barn.

"What were your instructions?" Trina asked as they walked the horses toward a gate leading into a wide meadow.

"I told Josie we needed a good hard ride."

"Excellent instructions." She leaned over as they reached the gate. "I'll get it." Once they were both through, she turned back and latched it again, moving with the agility of a woman used to dealing with gates while on a horse.

He glanced over at her. "You know, that hat makes you look about sixteen."

"That's how old it is. Mom still had it in the closet."

"Does it have a string to hold it on?"

"It does." Lifting the hat, she let the cord fall out and tightened it under her chin. "How about yours?"

"I'll hold it on."

"You can race one-handed?"

"Honey, I can race no-handed."

"Now *that's* the Hutch I remember. First one to the trees wins!" And she was off.

Hutch nudged Ink Spot into a gallop and chased her down. Once he caught up with her, he pulled back a little so they could race neck-and-neck toward the trees at the far side of the meadow. Judging from Ink Spot's response, Jack had given him the faster horse. Jack was that kind of friend, always wanting his buddies to look good in front of the ladies.

But Hutch had no desire to win this race. He was content to run beside Trina and watch her soaking up the thrill of the ride. She glanced over at him once and her smile was wide and happy, as if she'd forgotten everything but her love of riding full-out.

She hadn't looked very happy standing at the bottom of the stairs this morning. He hadn't been particularly happy, either. His dad could have told him *something*, at least, some little hint that life was about to change in a major way. And now Hutch had to end this thing with Trina when it had only just begun.

As they neared the tree line, he tightened the reins and let Trina win.

She whirled Patches around and waited for him while her horse pranced and snorted. "You pulled up, didn't you?"

"Who, me?"

"No fair." But she was laughing, so she couldn't be too upset.

"Let's walk them into the trees and grab some shade."

"Sounds good." She led the way along a narrow trail through dappled sunlight. Now that they were in partial shade, she'd slipped off her hat and let it hang down her back by the cord.

Sunbeams filtered through the trees and picked out the highlights in her glossy brown hair. Now he knew the joy of running his fingers through those soft strands. He knew the sweet smell of her hair, and how it felt sliding over his body while she... okay, maybe he'd better not think about that, because those moments were over.

But even if he squashed those thoughts, his heart was still captured by the beauty of the scene, and the beauty of the woman riding ahead of him. Now that they'd found each other, he hated like hell to give her up.

But he couldn't have casual sex with her anymore, not with his dad and her mother aware of it. They'd expect marriage plans, and that was out of the question. As a videographer, he was constantly on the move. As a trainer of racehorses, so was she. Neither of them should have to give up careers they loved so they could be together.

He edged into the subject sideways, resisting the idea of hitting it head-on. "So are we about to become related?"

She turned in the saddle. "Sort of, I guess. I should probably call Nash today and clue him in."

"Speaking of Nash, is there a chance we can keep him from finding out about last night?" If it would never happen again, no use getting his buddy riled up.

"I don't know. I won't say anything, but I can't guarantee the 'rents won't. They've become a couple of loose cannons."

"Tell me about it."

"Hutch, I'm getting a crick in my neck. Can we get down so we can have a proper discussion?"

"Sure." So this was it. He stopped his horse and she did the same. After they'd tied both sets of reins to a low-lying branch, he motioned to a fallen log. "Will that do?"

"It will." She sat down and patted the spot next to her.

"Maybe I should stand."

She gazed up at him. "Why?"

"Because the closer I get, the more I want to kiss you, and I think, under the circumstances, we need to..."

"Call a halt?"

He squeezed his eyes shut. "Damn it, I don't want to, but... yes. Our cover is blown. And if they're really getting married, we'll be seeing each other at family gatherings. You heard my dad. He doesn't approve of casual sex."

"I doubt my mother does, either."

"And then there's your brother. Technically Nash is fine with people having casual sex, but not if his little sister's the one having it, *especially* if you're having it with me. Am I right?"

She nodded. "Sadly you are."

"But our lives are too complicated and far apart for it to be anything else."

"I know. Normally I don't care what people think, but these people are our nearest and dearest. Carrying on an affair under their noses would seriously affect our relationship with them, so..." She sighed. "I guess we're done."

His jaw tightened in rebellion, but it seemed like the only way. "I guess we are." He did his best to ignore the gaping hole of sadness threatening to swallow him at the realization that he would never make love to her again.

"But our situation aside, I'm worried about you. Like I said before, I've had seven years to get over losing my dad, so this isn't a huge shock to me. But for you it's different. I can understand if you're having a tough time with the idea of your dad taking a new wife."

"Yeah." He stared at the pattern of leaves under his feet and thought about his mom. Then he remembered how lonely his dad had been for months. Lifting his head, he gazed at Trina. "You know what? I'm okay with Dad marrying your mom, although it seriously messes us up. He needs someone, and she obviously adores him. But I'm mad as hell that he didn't tell me what was going on."

"You have a right to be." Trina stood and came over to put her arms around him. "I think he was worried you wouldn't like it, but he should have told you. I'll bet if you give him a chance to apologize, he will."

"Maybe so." Once she nestled against him, he couldn't stop himself from wrapping her up tight and laying his cheek on her silky hair. "You feel so good."

"You, too."

"I'm going to really hate seeing you from time to time and not being able to hold you like this."

"I know. I'll hate it, too, but it's for the best."

"There'll be a big get-together at Christmas, I'll bet."

"Probably." She lifted her head and looked at him with dismay. "Do you think we're all supposed to stay in your dad's house? Including you, me and Nash?"

"Now there's an impossible situation. Sleeping down the hall from each other. Me, wanting you, and—"

"And me wanting you, yet we're not willing to carry on a tacky affair during the visit." Frustration creased her brow for many long seconds. Then, gradually, she began to smile. "There's only one solution."

"I can't imagine what. Trina, I'm not in a position to marry you and settle down, and I don't see you being ready to do that, either."

"I'm not. But what if we're not having an affair? What if we've committed to each other, but we don't know what shape that commitment will take yet? Everyone knows our lifestyles don't mesh, and we will acknowledge that, but we can tell them we're working it out the best we can for now. It's not a temporary affair. It's not casual sex. It's... a romance."

Hope flickered to life, easing his growing sense of despair. "I like the concept, but how can we work it out? For us, I mean, not the story we tell everyone."

"We'll have to be creative and somewhat unconventional. You'll be traveling and I'll be traveling, but what if we figure out how to match up here and there? Surely our schedules could be flexible enough for us to find the time to rendezvous."

Slowly his bruised heart began to revive. "You'd be okay with that? Grabbing weekends, never knowing for sure how often we'd get together?"

"If the alternative is swearing off you forever, I'd be more than okay with that. The thing is I seem to be falling in love with you, Langford Hutchinson."

That statement brought him so much happiness that he didn't even care that she'd used his real first name. "What a coincidence." He gazed into her eyes. "I seem to be falling in love with you, too, Katrina Bledsoe."

Smiling, she reached up to cup his face in both hands. "Then I think we should give ourselves a chance to explore that possibility, don't you?"

"Absolutely." He lowered his head. "Starting now." As he kissed her, he tasted the promise of all they would share in the coming months. If he had anything to say about it, they would fall so completely in love that time and distance would no longer matter. In fact, he could feel it happening already.

New York Times bestselling author Vicki Lewis Thompson's love affair with cowboys started with the Lone Ranger, continued through Maverick, and took a turn south of the border with Zorro. She views cowboys as the Western version of knights in shining armor, rugged men who value honor, honesty and hard work. Fortunately for her, she lives in the Arizona desert, where broad-shouldered, lean-hipped cowboys abound. Blessed with such an abundance of inspiration, she only hopes that she can do them justice.

For more information about this prolific author, visit her website and sign up for her newsletter. She loves connecting with readers.

VickiLewisThompson.com